THE

PROTECTOR'S SECRET;

OR,

THE PURITAN'S DAUGHTER.

A ROMANCE.

" Take away that bauble !"—CROMWELL.

London:

PUBLISHED BY E. LLOYD, 12, SALISBURY-SQUARE, FLEET-
STREET, AND SOLD BY ALL BOOKSELLERS.

THE PROTECTOR'S SECRET;
OR, THE PURITAN'S DAUGHTER.

CHAPTER I.

OLD LONDON.—THE NIGHT SEARCH.—THE CAPTURE.—AN APPEAL.

THE sun had sunk to rest some hours, and a cold blusterous wind, was sweeping through the streets of old London, in the year 1652, upon a night most memorable in the history of the kingdom, when dimly visible like a black floating mass upon the waters, a small boat was rowed from Whitehall towards the city.

The Thames was at high tide, and the water beat with a sullen roar, upon a long line of shingle that was at the back of the garden walls of the houses, that came down to the bank of the river.

There were four persons in the boat, two of those were soldiers, as their steel caps, cuirasses and arms sufficiently testified, and they sat apart from the other two, who were dressed as civilians, and who conversed together in eager whispers.

One of these was a tall fair haired man, of ingenuous aspect. The other was short and thick-set, of features almost repulsively ugly, and with a peculiar expression about the lower jaw, that gave a great character of ferocity to the whole face.

The fair man was Colonel Vernon, of Cromwell's own regiment of horse—the thick-set man was Oliver Cromwell himself.

" And so you think, Vernon, that this tale is a true one," whispered Cromwell, with something of a sneer.

" True enough," replied Vernon, " to be worth proving a mistake. Providence may this night throw into your hands him who would be a disturbance to you, and England, while he lived."

" Providence ! Vernon, the ways of Providence are mysterious, and therefore we will reserve mention of it, and its probable or possible interference with our affairs, for the multitude, who want such a guide star among clouds. We are men, and look to realities."

" Truly, general,"

" And so, Vernon——Ah ! whither are the knaves rowing ?"

The boatmen who made up the number of persons in the little wherry to six, which was quite as many as with any amount of safety it could carry, were passing the landing place near to Buckingham-street, which was the destination of the party.

" The tide, your honour," said one of the boatmen.

" Well. The tide ?"

" Why, your honour sees it runs like a mill stream here, and we must go past Croft's-castle a bit, to run in."

Cromwell gave one of those grunts, which he usually indulged in, when some statement was made to him which he had no means of disputing, and in a few moments the head of the boat was run in, towards a few wooden steps, that led to the garden of a large old rambling castellated mansion, called Croft's-castle, which there stood.

Colonel Vernon spoke a few words to the watermen, who nodded, and made the boat fast, after which, he and Oliver Cromwell, and the two soldiers who were dismounted troopers from the colonel's regiment, ascended the wooden steps, and pushing open a small gate, were fairly in the garden.

Cromwell's right hand was plunged into the breast of his apparel, and in all probability grasped some weapon. The cumbrous and clumsy fitting of his cloathing, sufficiently proclaimed the presence of defensive armour beneath it.

He turned completely round several times, as if to be quite sure that no one was close at hand.

" Should your cousin be right," said Cromwell to Vernon. " This will be a great night in English history."

" Indeed, general, it will."

" Aye, in more ways than one. We shall see. Come on, and mark me, troopers, if I raise my hand thus, fire your carbines into the breast of him towards whom my glance is fully directed. It will be the Lord's work ! Come on, Vernon. We should be compassionate, and charitable to our fellow creatures ; and so your cousin reports, that at night, one hour or so after sunset, a young cavalier in a boat by himself takes refuge here, but does not leave until near to sun rise, when he repairs on board the Dutch vessel, which we have already in vain searched."

" Even so."

" And that in appearance, he is like Charles ?"

" Yes, general."

"'Tis well. The old fox has fallen to the hunters. It will be well if we can unkennel the young one, and yet this man, who calls himself 'Walk-in-the-right-path Strangeways' has a good repute."

"The cant of religion, general, is a garb so accommodating, that any fool may wear it, how much easier must it be to a knave."

"Indeed. Ah! If the Lord be willing, we shall do wonders."

While Cromwell and his friend, are slowly and noiselessly making their way up the long garden of the house, which together with all its appurtenances was demolished long ago, we will take a glance at its interior and its inhabitants.

In a large gaunt-looking room sat Walk-in-the-right-path Strangeways, with his family, consisting of his wife and daughter—the former as prim and starched a piece of humanity as London could produce, and the latter as fair and gentle a looking creature, as the eye of day ever looked upon.

Mary Strangeways was indeed eminently loveable. She was sixteen years of age, but looked one year older. Surely it was some freak of nature, that bestowed upon such persons as the Strangeways, such a pure, fresh, guileless and beautiful creature, as Mary for a daughter.

Certainly she monopolised all that was good and gentle in Croft's-castle to herself entirely.

There was a visible agitation in Mary's manner, as she rose and approached her father and mother, to receive their blessing for the night. Strangeways fixed his little cold, grey eyes upon her, as he said,—

"Again this agitation and change of colour. The Lord be with us all!"

"Amen!" said Mrs. Strangeways.

"I thought," added the father, in a canting, puritanical tone, "I thought that when along with so many more of the ungodly, this city was rid of the malignant young man named Charles Courtney, that you would have turned your attentions as I wished you, to the pious Fear-no-man-in-the-gospel Muggs."

A shriek burst from Mrs. Strangeways, for the door of the room opened at this moment, and in rolled the one serving man of the family, looking the picture of consternation and dismay, while close upon his footsteps followed Cromwell, Vernon, and the two troopers.

Even Strangeways got up in his fright, and moving away two steps from his chair, sat upon the floor with the expectation of regaining it, as Cromwell, in a loud voice, said,—

"Stir not, on your lives. Do you know me?"

"The general?"

"Aye, Heaven's general. Vernon, can you amuse this pious family awhile, and I will please myself by looking through the ancient house with these two gospel-loving soldiers. Who knows but we may be repaid by finding some great curiosity?"

"Oh, no, no, no," cried Mary. "I, I—no, no."

Cromwell darted forward and grasped her by the wrist.

"Speak, maiden," he cried. "Speak as though you stood upon the shore of that sea which washes the eternal land. Speak."

Mary looked terrified, and well she might, at the vehemence of that man, who, when he chose to terrify, certainly possessed the art of doing so in no common degree. She did not, however, make any revelation which, on the impulse of the moment he expected and wished her to do.

"Go to," he said, as he cast her hand from him. "We must do the good work ourselves. Follow me."

These last words were addressed to the two troopers, and Oliver Cromwell, with them close upon his heels, moved towards a door which was opposite to that at which he had entered. Mary sprung after him.

"Sir," she said, "from what my father has said, I recognize in you General Cromwell."

"Well."

"What do you seek here?   What do you hope to find?"

He fixed his keen eyes upon her, and replied,

"What you and your parents, there, know is hidden."

"Nay, verily and truly," said Strangeways, gathering himself to his feet, "there is nought hidden here."

"Really.   Well, we will endeavour by an active and unscrupulous search to verify the words of so pious a man.   Remember, sir, this house is now on all points surrounded by sentinels upon whom I know I can depend.   Escape is impossible. Give up him whom I seek, and save your life.   If I have to find him, a military execution will be the reward of the harbourer of the man with the most dangerous name that can be uttered in England."

Walk-in-the-right-path Strangeways looked the picture of amazement, and in another moment Cromwell left the room. He was closely followed by Mary, despite the opposition of the troopers, and darting past the party, she dashed up a large oaken staircase at such speed that to stop her was impossible.

With a very irreligious kind of oath, Cromwell, closely followed by his two soldiers, pursued her.

"Charles, Charles," she cried.   "Fly, fly."

"By Heaven! he is here," shouted Cromwell.

A door was slammed shut in his face by Mary, and so sharply too that it actually struck him.   To dash himself against it and force it open was the work of a moment, and with the two soldiers he stood upon the floor of a small bed-room.

Mary was there with her hands clasped, and looking as though she had wrought up her mind to some great purpose.

"He is here," cried Cromwell.

"Oh, what has he done to you," said Mary, "that you should seek his life? What offence can he have committed against you?   Mercy and justice forbid you to harm him."

Cromwell looked round the room.   A light burnt upon a small bracket in the wall above the chimney-piece; opposite to it was a door connecting with a small closet.

One glance at the eyes of Mary sufficed to convince him—for in such matters he was sagacious beyond all ordinary sagacity—that it was in that closet some one was hidden.

That it was the object of his search he had little doubt, and if ever Cromwell thought himself upon the point of gaining possession of Charles the Second, he did upon this eventful evening.

"Fire into that closet," he said to the troopers.

The command was given with that stern deliberation with which he was accustomed to say things that he really meant.

Then two rough-looking carbines that the troopers carried with them were on the instant presented towards the door of the closet.   Another moment and they would have been discharged, had not Mary with a shriek of agony that even reached the ears of Colonel Vernon and her parents in the room, rushed forward, and flung herself before the door of the closet, so that if the soldiers had fired, there is little doubt but that she would have fallen a sacrifice to the bullets.

"No, no," she cried, "spare him.   Bold bad man that you are, Oliver Cromwell, I dare you thus to shed innocent blood.   Let the stain of human gore that is already upon thy soul suffice thee."

Cromwell's countenance turned of an ashy paleness, and he could only say, in a voice terribly indicative of suppressed passion,—

"This will be remembered.   You confess he is here?"

"Yes, yes."

"Charles?"

"Yes, Charles."

"Triumph, triumph!   This is the moment I have longed——"

The closet door opened from within, and a young man, of most strikingly handsome appearance, but very plainly attired, although his long hair, hanging in waving curls over his shoulders, proclaimed him a cavalier, made his appearance, and confronted Cromwell.

With a groan the Lord Protector, that was to be, stepped back.

"It is not he," he gasped, "it is not he!"

The closet was small, and a glance sufficed to convince Cromwell that no one else was there. In a voice now of thunder, he cried,—

"Who are you, malignant? Who are you, that have deceived the Lord's people, by assuming the character of that Charles who claims to be second king of his name, but who has been smitten down from his high place?"

"I assume no character but my own," said the young cavalier, proudly. "My name is Charles Courtney."

"Ha!" sneered Cromwell, "and the bed-chamber companion of Walk-in-the-right-path Strangeways' only daughter?"

"My husband," said Mary, with quiet dignity, as she entwined her arm in that of Charles Courtney, "my husband, sir. You are worse than ordinary intruders in this place."

CHAPTER II.

THE DISSOLUTION OF THE LONG PARLIAMENT.

OLIVER CROMWELL was accustomed to feel passion in its most stormy aspects, and now certainly he did look as though he were half choaked by the efforts he was compelled to make to preserve anything like an appearance, even of outward composure. But that, too, was a species of struggle to which he was tolerably well accustomed, and after a few moments, during which the perspiration stood in large drops like dew upon his brow, he turned and left the apartment.

The two troopers followed him closely. They saw what a mistake had been made, and they looked at each other like men who had been upon the verge of some great adventure, and then, by some common place juggle, were deprived of its results.

That any further use would be found now for their carbines they very much doubted, and one whispered to the other,—

"Truly, Dobsworth-in-the-faith, I would have spared my silver piece, had I been at all aware of how things would turn out."

"Your silver piece? What mean you?"

"Have you not heard that it has been said, that no bullet of lead will trouble the life of the second Charles?"

"I have of a surety heard so much."

"Then I put a bent silver noble into my carbine."

"A good thought. But it appears our general was mistaken."

Cromwell took his way direct to the room below, and addressing Colonel Vernon, he said,—

"We have wasted some precious time that might have been the Lord's. Let us hasten from here."

Vernon looked at the vexed countenance of Cromwell as he said, in a low tone,—

"Not here?"

"One Charles, but not of the coinage that will pass current." Then turning to Strangeways, he added, "Master Walk-in-the-right-path Strangeways, I give you joy—joy exceeding."

Strangeways looked perplexed, which seemed in some measure to restore Cromwell to a sort of ferocious good humour, and he added,—

"Yes, exceeding joy of a malignant, for a son-in-law. Your daughter keeps her gallants close at hand, and in the atmosphere of this house, which has been represented to me as full of aspirations for the well-being of the state, there float royalist prayers and royalist feelings enough to waft the second Charles to St. James's."

"You amaze me," said Strangeways.

He was not however, for a long time left to the amazement of his own conjectures, for the door of the room opened again, and Charles Courtney made his appearance, with Mary upon his arm.

"Behold," said Cromwell.

Strangeways started to his feet, and Charles advancing said,—

"Sir, that I have done you some wrong in making your child my wife, which event took place some weeks since, I freely confess, I can make but one reparation, and that is, to love her, and to cherish her as my life."

"Father! Father!" said Mary.

She would have flung herself upon his neck, but he thrust her rudely from him, exclaiming,—

"My sword, my sword! The sword of Gideon.—My sword, that I may slay the malignant!"

He darted to a corner of the apartment, where among a quantity of miscellaneous articles were several swords—grasping one, he returned, and was about to strike at Charles Courtney, when Cromwell strode between them.

"The fool," he said, "striketh his own face, to slay the fly that tickles him. Be more wise in your generation, Master Strangeways."

"The sword of Gideon!" exclaimed the puritan. "I will smite the malignant."

"The sword of a fool!" cried Cromwell, as he with one vigorous movement, disarmed Strangeways. Then turning to Colonel Vernon, he said,—"Follow me, we have that to do to-night, which brooks not more delay."

Without casting another look on the parties assembled, he walked from the room, Colonel Vernon followed him, and the two troopers who had waited just without the door, brought up the rear.

The boat was soon gained, and Cromwell making a sign with his hand that he wished to go towards Westminster, sat for some time in gloomy silence, with his arms across his breast.

They landed at an obscure stairs at the back of Whitehall.

"Hark!" cried Cromwell.

"What do you hear?" said Vernon.

"A voice which bids me do that to-night, which will be gracious in the sight of all who wish well to this realm. Our parliament has long enough desecrated the place in which it sits, and forgotten the objects of its sitting. This way, Vernon. I must, after some prayer, do that to-night which it is right should be done."

"The long parliament is doomed," muttered Colonel Vernon to himself.

*   *   *   *   *   *   *

At the moment Cromwell was uttering these words, so darkly indicative of what was brooding at his heart, to Colonel Vernon, Sir Harry Vane was addressing the House of Commons in that long parliament, which in its tortuous and vacillating career, had alternately lauded and deprecated the acts of Cromwell.

The house was unusually full of members, and Sir Harry had an attentive audience, as he uttered the following words.

"Is it not more necessary that a House of Commons should command a successful general, and point to him where and in what quarters to exert his powers, than that he, assuming to himself a deliberative as well as an executive condition, should wage his own wars, concoct his own expeditions, and keep us sitting here for no earthly purpose but to vote him subsidies."

Loud cries of "Hear! Hear!" welcomed the opinions of Sir Harry. To be sure there were some members who looked uneasy, because they were far-sighted enough to foresee the collision that was almost sure to take place sooner or later, between Cromwell and the Commons, but these were few in comparison to those who were angry at the assumed authority of Cromwell, and who would gladly have adopted some mode of cutting down the pretensions and the insolence of the victorious general.

A desultory debate followed, in the course of which many members expressed themselves with more freedom than discretion concerning the acts of Cromwell, and several went the length of saying, that they had no doubt but that his ambition looked much further than it was at all, by the generality of persons, imagined to be possible.

Sir Harry Vane rose again, and said,—

"The question, Mr. Speaker, resolves itself into this—is Oliver Cromwell to be the general of this House of Commons, or is this House of Commons to be the mere treasurers of Oliver Cromwell? I apprehend that our object is the protection of our own independence."

"Hear! hear! hear!"

At this moment, all eyes were directed towards the door below the bar of the House. It was evident that there was something amiss, for some cries of pain were heard, and the sounds as of some struggle going on.

Whatever it was, however, it was of very short duration, for the door of the House was flung open, and Oliver Cromwell, accompanied only by Colonel Vernon, entered it.

For a few moments, during which Cromwell marched up to the table of the House, every one seemed too much taken by surprise to speak. Then a single voice called,—

"Privilege! privilege!"

Cromwell had reached the table, and with his clenched hand resting upon it, he turned hastily in the direction whence the sound came. Sir Harry Vane rose from his seat, and, with violence of manner, cried,—

I denounce this invasion of the house. I call upon the Speaker to order the arrest of this contumacious servant of the state."

"Oh, Sir Harry Vane—Sir Harry Vane," said Cromwell, lifting up his hand, "God keep me from Sir Harry Vane."

"Traitor!" cried a member.

"Traitor!" shouted Cromwell, in a voice that rang through the house, "you are all rank traitors. You have sat here long enough. Give place to honester men. I dissolve this parliament in the name of the people."

Every member present rose to his feet, and for a few moments the war of words was overwhelming. A partial rush was made towards Cromwell, but at that moment, by a preconcerted signal, there marched into the House a compact, well-chosen, and fully armed body of three hundred soldiers.

"Give place, I say," cried Cromwell; "this is no longer a place for any of you."

The Speaker rose and tried to speak, but Cromwell turned upon him such a look of fierceness that he shrunk back, but he pointed, or seemed to point, to the huge gilt mace which lay upon the table.

"Take away that bauble," cried Cromwell.

A war of rage and execration came from the members of the house. Cromwell's eyes seemed to flash fire as he waved his arm, crying,—

"Disperse, ye men of Belial, disperse!"

The soldiers pressed forward, and began to use their weapons roughly. A scene of terrific confusion ensued. Some of the members broke through the ranks of the military, and without their hats, fled from the house. Others climbed to the galleries, and sought more obscure modes of exit; while some dropped from the windows, being under an impression that it was the intention of Cromwell to slaughter them all.

Again he waved his arm, and the soldiers pressed more energetically upon the few members who seemed disposed to make a stand. They were so few, however, that it would have been madness for them to persevere in a hopeless resistance.

In a wonderfully short space of time, therefore, the hall was cleared, and the long parliament was dissolved.

Cromwell looked beneath his bushy brows at Colonel Vernon, and said,—.

"It is the Lord's work. Let those doors be closed until honester men be found to enter them. Truly this shall be a great deliverance to the people of this land.

Colonel Vernon's face was flushed, for he knew the full hazard, and the full importance of the step that Cromwell had taken.

"It shall be done," he replied. "Truly this is a great work."

"It is a work, Vernon, which shall be spoken of long after you and I are with those who speak no more."

"I do not doubt it, general."

"Now," continued Cromwell, "the work of regeneration of this country can be proceeded with, and the puppet called a prince must follow the puppet called a king."

"They call him now the second Charles."

"Bah! did ever the circlet of royalty encompass his brows? Did ever the velvet and ermine of kingly state encumber his limbs?"

"No; and yet——"

"And yet what?"

"Those who madly espoused his cause called him king the moment that the gory head of the first Charles——"

"No more of that," said Cromwell, "no more of that. I have here," striking his heart, "a better picture of that gory head than you can paint to me. Enough, enough, I say. This king of phantoms and of shadows whom you speak of, will fall as fell his progenitor, and wanting a name ready at hand as the cloak for faction, let us hope that faction will expire. I—I do not know the time. Is it near the dawn?"

"No, general, not by hours."

"Come with me, Vernon, I—I almost think——"

"What?"

"That—I—I will entrust you with a secret; yet—no—no—no."

A perceptible shudder ran through the frame of Cromwell, and without evidently knowing what he was about, he kept on saying,—

"No—no—no—no."

"At your good pleasure," said Vernon.

"Eh! what of my good pleasure?"

"The secret you thought of communicating to me."

"Secret!—a dream—a dream—a dream. Let us hasten. What a gloomy bit of road is this."

"It is so, general."

The soldiers had been left to a subordinate command, and Cromwell, with Colonel Vernon, had walked as far as the corner of Westminster-bridge, where, at that period, a narrow tortuous thoroughfare commenced, and continued for some distance towards Whitehall.

It well enough merited the appellation of gloomy which Cromwell had given to it.

As they passed a narrow gateway, which seemed to be the entrance to some sort of ship-building yard, a man darted out, and, with a short stout poinard, made a blow at the breast of Cromwell.

So well directed, and so sudden was the attack, that the point of the dagger struck him so fully and fairly upon the breast as the assassin could wish it to do; but the weapon broke sharply off at the hilt, and the blade, after hanging one brief moment entangled in Cromwell's clothes, fell to the ground.

It seemed as though the dagger had been struck against a man composed of steel.

"Thanks, good corslet," said Cromwell, as he staggered back from the sheer force of the blow.

Colonel Vernon happened to have a heavy steel gauntlet upon his right hand, and without pausing to draw his sword, he dealt the assassin such a blow upon the face with it, that he fell, deluged with blood and perfectly insensible at their feet.

"It is over," said Cromwell ; " I felt it was coming, it is over."

" The villain is foiled," said Vernon.

" Yes, yes, the Lord fights with his soldiers ; Vernon, is he dead ?"

" No general, he has had no vital injury from me."

" Vernon, this man was hired."

" Doubtless."

" Well, Vernon, a hired assassain failed, and punished becomes a personal foe, full of dire revenges.

" I should fancy so much."

" Those who by the Lord's grace are set up in high places, Vernon, are special works for the insane and the turbulent. Attempts like these are best neither talked of nor publicly punished. What may we do with this man ?"

Vernon was silent. He began to comprehend what Cromwell meant.

"Our swords," he said, "have been drawn too often in holy causes to stoop to execute a ruffian like this. The river runs close at hand."

"A lucky thought," said Cromwell.

While thus insensible it were but mercy to cast him into the stream—a far less punishment than his crime would warrant, or than the law would condemn him to.

Colonel Vernon was a man of great personal strength, and stooping for a moment over the prostrate form of the assassin, he ran with him in his arms towards the bridge.

Cromwell followed.

They met but one passenger, and he knowing how out of joint the times were, thought it prudent to get out of the way, so he crossed the road, and turned out of danger. In those days, the safest thing was always not to see that which did not immediately concern you.

The assassin betrayed no sign of consciousness. The blow which Colonel Vernon had given him with the iron gauntlet, had been sufficiently severe to produce a long state of syncopes, and if the wretch had been permitted to live, would have sent him forth into the world again, maimed and marked for the remainder of his existence.

The colonel reached the first arch of the bridge. A glance into the stream shewed him that the water was at its utmost height.

"Farewell, my friend," he said as he launched the assassin over the parapet. " You will trouble the state no more."

There was a plunge, and then all was still.

When Colonel Vernon turned round to speak to Cromwell, he, to his surprise, found that he was gone.

CHAPTER III.

THE NIGHT BRAWL IN THE STRAND.

It is now past midnight, and from the cloudy sky the moon tries in vain to peep down upon England.

The miserable oil lamps that at long intervals from each other, lend a dim light to the streets of London, are doing their best, although it was always doubtful if positive darkness was not absolutely preferable to their uncertain and flickering rays.

In the Strand, which even then was considered quite a gay and sportive sort of characterised thoroughfare, a greater attempt was made to light up than anywhere else, and hence, probably, arose partly the custom of more night brawls taking place in that locality than elsewhere in olden London.

To be sure there was another reason that contributed, no doubt, to make the Strand a scene of popularity, as regarded those witless youths who found amusement in disturbing the rest of the soberer portion of the congregation.

That reason was to be found in the vicinage of the Thames.

Nothing could be more convenient than to run down one of the narrow sloping streets that led to the river, jump into a boat, and for a few pence be landed, if need were, upon the other side of the water.

The Strand then, from Temple-Bar to Somerset-House in particular, was the scene of many brawls, which kept the shop keepers in a constant fret.

On this night in particular it seemed as though some score of devils had been let loose in the thoroughfare.

"Dashall? Dashall, I say!" cried Mrs. Dashall, the by far the better half of a well-to-do draper in the Strand. "Dashall, you monster! Will you date to pretend to be asleep, while the door is being knocked down? Dashall, I say! Oh I'll let you know to-morrow that I am not to be trifled with in this way. So you won't wake?"

"My dear," said Dashall meekly, "I am awake."

"Oh, you are, are you? very well, sir, then perhaps you are aware that the door is being battered down."

"I hear a noise."

"You hear a noise, you mean-spirited, cowardly wretch, you hear a noise. Yes, indeed, but you do not stir. Dashall, I do believe if you were to wake up and find two men in the bed, you would only say you heard a noise."

"Two men in the bed, my dear, what an idea! How our niece, Jemima, must be frightened. Dear me, there is a knocking to be sure."

"Yes, our niece, Jemima, indeed. Your niece, you mean—not my niece—I won't have anything to say to her, and I only wonder at myself for allowing this house to be made an alms-house for your poor relations."

"Dear me!"

"Oh, you odious wretch! you ain't half a man. That's the fact, you ain't half a man, Dashall."

"Very well, my dear."

"But it ain't very well, now are you going to get up and go down stairs to find out what that row is?"

"Oh, if you wish it."

"If I wish it? If I wish it? when here for half an hour I have been, quite begging of you to do so. Dashall, Dashall, you are certainly one of the most impracticable of men, that you are."

"Well, I'm going."

Dashall got up, for he had no more idea of disobeying the mandates of Mrs. Dashall than of attempting with his shop ladder to step up to the moon; he soon procured a light, and enveloping himself in a morning wrapper, he crept slowly down stairs.

"I know it will turn out to be nothing," he said to himself, "but it's of no use saying as much to Mrs. D. Ah, its a pity she's rather violent, for what a fine woman, and what a clever woman she is."

Bang, bang, bang! went the knocker of the door, and then some half-a-dozen dissolute young men who were there held a brief consultation."

"They won't open it," said one, "and the watch will be here directly."

"Oh, they are sure to come; however, hammer away Joceylin, you must find shelter somewhere you know, for you will be recognised else most assuredly. You put that fellow who drew upon you out of all earthly trouble."

"I think I killed him," said Joceylin.

"And, therefore, you must be housed somewhere for an hour—we have never yet found this plan fail. Oh, there is a light."

The faint glimmer of the light carried by Dashall as, in obedience to his lady's imperious commands, he crept down to the door, was visible through the fan-light of coarse blue glass above it.

"Now for it, knock away."

He who was by his companion named Joceylin, hammered away at the street door of the draper's house, and just as he did so, a strong body of the watch appeared some distance off, but coming along as fast as they could in the direction of the rioters.

Dashall opened the door, and stood shivering upon the threshold with the candle in his hand.

"Gentlemen, cavaliers," he said, "really, I——"

"Oh, my dear friend," said one, rushing towards him and dragging him on to the pavement by a vigorous grasp of the hand.

"My old and valuable acquaintance," said another as he blew out the light.

"My fine and fast rollicking jovial companion," said a third.

"Gentlemen, gentlemen," said poor Dashall, "I—I, really—"

He was pulled in one direction by one—in another direction by another—while a third twisted him right round, and then, as if by magic, or as though they were all seized by some extraordinary and sudden impulse at the same period of time, they ran off and made their way down a side street that lead to the Thames.

During the time, however, that the draper had been so mystified by so many persons, of whom he knew nothing, claiming acquaintance with him, the young man named Jocylin had slipped into his house.

"Bless me, what is the meaning of it all?" said Dashall. "I suppose, after all, it was only some freak. Upon my life, its cold here, I'll—I'll go to bed again, and tell Mrs. D. that its all right."

Mr. Dashall entered his own passage again, and was about to close the street-door, when the watch arrived at the spot.

"Have you seen anybody pass, sir?" said one of the constables.

"Anybody?" cried Dashall. "I've seen a dozen bodies at least, and they knocked at my door till my wife made me—I mean till I got up and came down, and then they all pretended they knew me."

"Indeed?"

"Aye, indeed. Good night."

"Did you recognise any of them?"

"I recognised a set of wild night brawlers? No, Mr. Watchman, I can tell you my acquaintance don't lie among such a lot."

"No offence, sir."

"Oh, no—no—no."

Mr. Dashall closed his door, and put up a chain and a bar, and then shot two bolts into their sockets, as he said—

"Ah, I think now Mrs. D. will confess I am a man of courage, rather. Ah, this is something like, I actually almost bullied the watch. Come—come. Keep away from my door. You have mistaken your man. I'll soon make mince meat of you. Ha!"

Mr. Dashall amused himself as he walked up stairs by talking thus to a purely imaginary foe, but he wisely lowered his voice, and finally lapsed into absolute silence as he approached within ear shot of Mrs. Dashall, who might not perhaps approve of the defiant disposition of her husband.

"What do you mean?" cried Mrs. Dashall.

"Mean, my dear? By what?"

"Why by going up and down stairs in that sort of way?"

"Bless me, my dear, you sent me down."

"Yes. But you have been up and down again. You came into the room, and when I spoke to you, you only went down again."

"Good gracious, it wasn't me!"

"Not you?" cried Mrs. Dashall, with a scream. "Then some strange cat—I mean man is in the house. Oh, you wretch, that's the way you protect me, is it. Oh, you odious monster!"

"But, my dear," said Dashall, as he stood trembling with fear and irresolution. "But, my dear."

"Don't dear me, sir.   There's no saying what might have happened, not that I think you would have cared, you mean-spirited wretch.   Oh, no!"

"But, my dear!"

"Oh—oh.   I feel my hysterics coming on."

"Stop 'em—stop 'em!   I'll get the brandy bottle in a moment."

"Oh—oh—oh."

"Now don't—don't, my dear.   You may depend it's all imagination.   There's no man in the house.   There's only me, it's all imagination."

"You know I never had any imagination.   Where's the bottle?"

"Here, my dear, here."

"How can you think, in my state of mind, that I can drink anything.   Oh, you are a wretch, you know you are, Mr. D.   That ever I should have thrown myself away upon such an animal.   I know there's somebody in the house.   Look under the bed."

Mr. Dashall gave a jump, for the possibility of there being any one under the bed set him all of a tremble again.   Nevertheless, in obedience to the mandate of his imperious spouse, he did look.

"There's nobody there, my dear, I assure you," he said.   "Now do be calm, I'm quite sure there's nobody in the house."

"I don't know that."

"But my love."

"Hush!"

Mr. Dashall was quieted in a moment, and listened with what folks call his ears. He thought he heard some faint noise in the house, but what it was, or where exactly it came from he could not say.

"Did you hear anything?" said Mrs. Dashall.

"Oh, dear, no," said Dashall, as he stole quietly to the door and locked it. How should I, my dear, when I know there is nobody in the house."

"Then," said Mrs. Dashall, "I shall get up and look myself, and you shall carry the candle."

A scream at this moment came upon their ears; Mrs. Dashall sprung out of bed, and Mr. Dashall most mysteriously disappeared under it—then unfortunately he dropped the light, and the room was in instantaneous darkness, so that Mrs. Dashall was brought to a complete stand still until she could procure a light, at all events.

Then there was all the groping about for the tinder-box, and then no end to trouble in getting an intractable piece of flint to emit a single spark.   After that, the tinder was decidedly damp, and then the matches were wet, and so that there was a good ten minutes fume and fret before Mrs. Dashall was rewarded by a faint blue light at the end of a match, by the aid of which she was to re-illumine the candle.   Of course, the candle had fallen in the very worst way it could, as it is the invariable habit of candles to do, and the wick was buried in an ocean of half congealed fat.   All this was, however got to rights by degress, and then Mrs. Dashall, with the candle in her hand, went to the door, when it was instantaneously blown out by somebody who was on the landing, and who said,—

"The light of your eyes, my dear madam, is amply sufficient to banish all the darkness in this house."

CHAPTER V

THE CAVALIER AND THE SPY.—THE GOOD ADVICE.

WE must now, for a brief space, leave Mrs. Dashall to all her fears, and to all her conjectures, regarding the uttering of this gallant remark, while we briefly recount to the reader how it was that the cavalier, who had thought proper to take refuge in Dashall's house, had got into the serious predicament, that rendered such a refuge at all neccessary. From a house in Fleet-street, contiguous to a tavern, the sign of which had been altered from the King's Head to the Boar's Head, there came two persons, one of whom was the young cavalier, who had taken refuge in the draper's house. The most earnest conversation was going on between them in whispers, until they got some short way through Temple-bar, when the taller of the two suddenly paused, and said,—

"Have you about you as much as a thousand pounds in jewels?"

The younger man looked amazed, and replied,—

"Certainly not. You know that I left the small casket at Harrison's."

"Then you are my prisoner."

"Indeed—a spy."

The taller man had drawn his sword, and made a blow at his younger companion, but the nimbleness of the latter saved him, and the other, having slightly over-reached himself, was near stumbling. The moment that it took him to recover his footing was fatal to him. The young cavalier drew a remarkably small but highly tempered rapier from its sheath, and ran him through in a moment. The spy, for such he was, writhed like an eel, and uttered a shriek, after which he fell heavily, half upon the pavement and half in the road-way.

"Good God, what a peril," said the young man. But he had not a long time for consideration as to what he had to do, for a party of the watch having heard the cry of the man who had suffered, justly enough, for his meditated treachery, came quickly up with their bills and staves. There was nothing for the young cavalier but instant flight, and he ran down the Strand as quickly as he could.

He had not proceeded far when he heard some voices singing in boisterous strains, one of the old Charlie airs, and he soon came dimly in sight of a party of young men, who, the moment they observed him, spread themselves in a line exactly in his way, crying,—

"Stop him. Stop him and make him drink the king's health at the pump. Stop the cropped knave. Stop him!"

"Gentlemen," said he who was pursued, dashing in among them. "We are of kindred feelings—I have had the misfortune to sheath my sword in an enemy of King Charles's, and the watch are upon my track."

"It it is so, you have fallen into good company," said one. "Draw, gentlemen, draw."

"Let's look at him by the lamp," said another. "Fair words, you know, gentlemen, all butter, no parsnips, and its easy for old Nal himself, in difficulty, to cry God save King Charles."

"Is this open language discreet, gentlemen?" said the young cavalier, who was now rather unceremoniously dragged into the dim glare from one of the street lamps.

"Discreet or not discreet, you are no puritan."

"And we have had a skinful of good canary," said another.

"But, gentlemen, let me beg of you to be sage in your cups."

"Your name—your name, stranger. What is your name?"

"Joceylin, they call me. Marmaduke Joceylin."

"A good name."

"The watch—the watch!" cried one. "Here they come. Over the river, friend Joceylin'; we will find you a place of safety.

"Nay, gentlemen," said Joceylin, "I may not go far from here. Can I not find some temporary place of shelter until the alarm is over?"

A brief consultation took place, and then it was determined to play the audacious trick that we have seen practised upon Dashall the draper, by making his house a temporary refuge for the young cavalier.

"Gentlemen cavaliers," he said, "I should like to know some of you upon some better occasion."

"You may know us all. We are templars. If you call at the lodge by the gate at Whitefriars for Master Rignold, you will find us all in due time, and we may find an opportunity of drinking a bumper to King Charles, and down among the dead men with the Puritans."

" We shall meet again."

" In good time.   Farewell."

In a few moments after this, Joceylin had found his way into the draper's house, and finding the first door he came to upon the ground-floor was locked, he had mounted the staircase, and found his way, unfortuately, into the draper's bedroom.

Mrs. Dashall, therefore, was perfectly right, when she had declared that some one came into the room to whom she had spoken, notwithstanding Mr. Dashall chose to think, or affected to choose to think that it was all to be ascribed to her too lively imagination.

"Confound it," said Joceylin, to himself. "They lock up their empty rooms, where one can do no harm, and leave open the chambers into which, just now, at least, one has no wish to penetrate."

He then thought that he surely must have passed some doors that might be open, and he descended a few steps, but before he could get far, he found that Mr. Dashall, who had procured a light again by some means, down stairs, was again ascending.

" These people will give me no peace," he said, and then seeing another flight of stairs above him, he sprang up without any other motive than that of getting out of Dashall's way.

He had not got far up this second flight of stairs, when he saw by a faint halo that came from under a door, that there was a light in some room.

He hesitated for some few moments as to whether or not he should go into that room.   He listened intently at the door of it, and heard no sound.

" All is still," he said.   " Perhaps no one is here.   At all events, desperate circumstances develope desperate resolves, I may find a friend."

He slowly opened the door of the room and peeped in.   It was a bed chamber, and the light was a small rush one, and burnt upon a little table by the window. The bed was at the farther end of the room, and it was so much shaded by a curtain, most probably to exclude the light from the eyes of the sleeper, that Josceylin could not come to any sort of conclusion as to who occupied it.   Curiosity, however, and some idea from the appointments of the room that it was tenanted by a young female, got the better of all prudence, and he advanced slowly on tiptoe towards the bed.   With the utmost caution and gentleness he removed the curtain so as to admit a ray of light to fall upon the sleeper, and then he looked upon the calm and serene countenance of a young girl in deep repose.   A lace cap had fallen off, and some luxuriant tresses of fair golden-looking hair had escaped from their confinement and wantoned over the cheek and neck of the guileless sleeper. For some few moments Joceylin looked at her in silence.   Then in a low tone he said,—

" She is very beautiful,"

He moved the curtain a little more so as to get a better light upon her face, but the sleeper was disturbed and moved slightly.   Joceylin dropped the curtain, and shadows fell once more upon the fair face.   She murmured something in her sleep, and bending forward to listen, he heard her pronounce the name of Alfred twice.   There was no mistaking the tone in which the name was uttered.

" Happy Alfred," said the young cavalier, when he was quite assured that sleep had once more come over the young maiden.   " Happy Alfred !"

As one of his excuses for making his way into that room he had endeavoured to tell himself that Dashall might be close upon his heels, but now that excuse no longer sufficed him, and yet he lingered.   It was the spell of youth and beauty that held him to the spot.   He felt as if he could have lingered hours looking upon that picture of youth and innocence.   And yet the circumstances of that young cavalier were truly desperate.   His life hung upon a thread, and all his hopes and aspirations at that time seemed buried in the tomb.   Surely the weight of many cares was upon his brow, and yet there he stood in the attic of Dashall the draper's house, looking his heart away at his pretty neice, Jemima, as she slept all unconscious of the admiration she was exciting.

"When shall I sleep as sound?" he said.

The necessity for moving from where he was, however, began to make itself manifest to him, and yet he could not leave without one tribute to the charms of Jemima of a more substantial character than the mere registry in his heart that she was beautiful.

"If I could snatch one kiss," he said, "without awakening her? Surely so gentle a disturbance will not rudely bid her slumbers vanish. One, only one. Ye loves be propitious and fan her to double repose."

Gently he leant over the little, humble couch, and pressed his lips for one brief moment to those of Jemima. She opened her eyes and looked at him with such utter bewilderment, that he thought perhaps another kiss might——Gracious Heavens, no. What a scream! He almost fell backwards, but he luckily dashed the light out with his left hand, and crying,—"It's only Alfred," he left the room. It was on his progress down stairs, that he blew Mrs. Dashall's light out, just as she made her appearance at the door of her chamber.

"Murder! murder! Fire!" shrieked Mrs. Dashall, when she found that there was really somebody in the house more than its legitimate occupants, and that that somebody preferred being without a light.

"Help! help! Murder!"

"Fire!" cried Dashall, from under the bed, as he stretched out his hand, and nervously clutched Mrs. Dashall by the ancle.

"To the devil with you all," said the cavalier as he ran down the stairs, and reached the passage in an exceedingly short space of time.

Dashall, however, without the least idea of premeditating such a thing, had effectually fastened his shop door, and in the dark the cavalier could not, for the life of him, find how the bar was fastened. He fumbled at it, and cursed it, and blessed himself, and stamped, and laughed, and then swore again, but all would not do. Suddenly a faint light came into the passage through the fanlight, and a voice from without, said, "I think I can manage it, and if the dying man's information be correct, we shall make a good thing of this affair."

"Yes," said another voice, but as we are only two, the grand thing will be to get the draper's family to help us. If you can find out his bed room, and let him know who is secreted in his house, all may be well."

"But wont he want to share?"

"Oh, confound him!"

"Well, well, get in. Cut away as much of the fanlight as you can."

Joceylin retreated until he at first fancied he had run against some one, but it was only a large great-coat of Dashall's that hung in the passage. "A prize!" said Joceylin to himself. In a moment he took it down, and by doing so, he brought down a cap that hung upon the same peg. "Well," he said, "how true it is, that the fates never effectually shut one door against a man, but what they open another. Who would know me as I now shall be disguised."

Another half minute sufficed to envelop him in the great-coat and cap. As for the coat, it was to him truly a great coat, for Mr. Dashall, though a fly in spirit, was an ox in proportions. He heard the man who had mounted up to the fanlight above the street door, cutting away the glass, and by the light of a lantern which he held to guide his operations, Joceylin was enabled to find out how the chain of the door, was fastened. That once down, and the door yielded. He opened it sharply, crying as he did so, "Help—help! Watch—watch."

"Here! here!" said the two men.

"There's a man up stairs under my bed," said Joceylin. "I'm all of a tremble. He's a cavalier."

"Yes—yes. Wait here for us. We will soon rid you of him, Mr. Dashall."

"Many thanks."

"Which is the room?"

"The first door to the right after you get on the landing. He seems a desperate fellow, and I must confess I am not used to fighting."

"How should you be? Lend us a light."

"You will find one up stairs."

"All's right—all's right. You keep guard at the door, in case he should chance to slip past us."

"Trust me for that."

The two men rushed up stairs with the greatest possible precipitation. Who or what they were, the cavalier never stopped to inquire. All he knew or cared to know concerning them, was that their manifest object was to make him prisoner. With all the speed he could muster he ran towards the city, and when near to Temple-bar, he disencumbered himself of the large great-coat belonging to Dashall, for it nearly smothered him. Just as he was about throwing it from him, a watchman rushed out of an entry, crying, "Stop thief!"

Joceylin cast the coat over the head of the man, who could not free himself from it until the young cavalier had darted through Temple-bar. There was something of a watch always kept at Temple-bar, but it was a lazy and inefficient one, having degenerated into a thing of form and fashion merely, so that the cavalier easily passed on. To be sure a weak effort was made to stop him, but a man with a drawn sword, and in a manifest hurry, is not the most desirable personage to stop in a sudden and uncourteous manner, so they let him pass on. He ran until he came to the next door to the tavern with the accommodating sign, and then with the hilt of his sword he struck repeatedly on the door. No attention was immediately paid to him, and feeling impatient, he ran into the roadway, and picking up a pebble, he flung it against one of the casements. A smash of broken glass ensued, and in another moment the door was opened cautiously, and a man looked out. "Sir Robert!" cried the cavalier.

"Gracious Heavens, is this possible?" said the man.

"True, if not possible," replied the cavalier, with a laugh. "I hope there are no more traitors than one in the camp."

"Traitors! Has Oxenden been false?"

"False as ———, but he lies in the Strand as fully as he ever lied in the city. Let me in."

During this brief parley, he who was called Sir Robert, and who had opened the door, had quite unwittingly filled up the small space, through which the young cavalier might have passed, but now, when called to a consciousness of what he was about, he moved aside with alacrity enough. The cavalier bounded into the passage of the dingy-looking house, for such indeed it was, and in another moment the door was diligently fastened by Sir Robert.

CHAPTER VI.

THE GREY VISITOR TO ST. JAMES'S.

It will be recollected that Oliver Cromwell had disappeared from the company of Colonel Vernon in a most mysterious manner, when the assassin was plunged into the river Thames. He had been following the colonel at about the distance of some half dozen paces, when from the shadow as it seemed of a deep doorway, there all at once emerged a figure which attracted all his attention, as it crossed his path. A slight gesture made by the figure, showed that there was some sort of intelligence between them. Cromwell hesitated only for a moment, and then striking his breast, he uttered a deep groan, after which he followed the figure having apparently, in the absorbing interest that it created in his mind, quite forgotten Colonel Vernon and the assassin. It is worth while, as this mysterious acquaintance of Cromwell's passes the few oil lamps in the route down towards

THE GREY VISITOR, FOLLOWED BY CROMWELL, PASSING THE SENTINELS.

St. James's, which was the one it took, to notice its peculiarities. A tall, slender form, was attired in a closely fitting dress of grey elastic cloth, the colour was of a particularly dull and uniform discription, and the dress itself was plain to a degree. A cloak of precisely the same colour hung about him, on his head he wore a strange conical kind of cap, which was likewise grey, and strange to say, his face bore a livid hue, which was very nearly allied to the colour of his garments. Such was the man, or something more or less than man, who strode before Cromwell in silence, and whom he followed with a species of insane fascination, which he could not shake off. Once only as the man was passing Whitehall, Cromwell spoke to him, and it was in a tone that shewed some strong feelings were at work within his breast.

"Has the time come," he said, "when all will be revealed to me ? Has the time come, I ask ? Tell me if the time has come ?"

An impatient gesture with one arm was the only notice the mysterious looking personage took of the impassioned interrogatory, and then he passed on rather more quickly than before. Cromwell at that time, had, for the convenience of being in a central and well-known position for his military operations, taken up his abode at St. James's, and it was towards the general's quarters in that building that the grey man now made his way. When they got close to one of the great gates, the stranger paused, and allowed Cromwell to come up with him. He then pointed significantly to the sentinel, who, in his heavy half armour, was pacing slowly to and fro. Cromwell understood him, and taking now the lead, he walked up to the gate. The sentinel saluted him, and Cromwell pausing a moment, and giving a slightly perceptible shudder, said,—

"This person is to pass always."

The voice of the sentinel saluting the general, brought out the captain of the guard, to whom Cromwell spoke, repeating the same words, while the grey man stood, tall and gaunt, looking like an apparition, in the dim light from the guard room. Something like surprise sat upon the officer's countenance, but he bowed his acquiescence in the command of his superior, and looked hard at the grey man, as though he would have said,—

"And am I to have no other means of recognition of this privileged person, but such as arise from the observations that I can make in these few fleeting moments ?"

The grey man seemed as though he read in the countenance of the officer, the thoughts that he did not give utterance to, for he suddenly advanced and letting the cloak which was gathered round him, fall from his face and the upper part of his person, the light of a lanthorn which a subaltern officer appeared with, fell full upon him.

"You will not forget him," said Cromwell.

"Never," said the officer, as he drew back, apparently both amazed and a little terrified at the apparition.

Cromwell gave a groan and passed on. The grey man gathered his cloak again about him, and followed. The guard at the gate of St. James's looked aghast. Well might they do so, when for the first time they saw him, whom they had been taught to consider as inflexible and immovable by all human passion, trembling and looking the very picture of superstitious dismay.

"This is strange," remarked the officer to the subaltern.

"More than strange," was the reply.

"Well, all we have to do is to obey orders, but I must confess, that the seldomer this grey man comes here, while I hold the post, the better I shall be pleased, for I do not at all like the looks of him."

"Nor I."

"Well, well, we live in strange times, so we ought not perhaps to be surprised at strange things happening in them. Should you know the man again, sentinel, who is to pass unquestioned ?"

"I shall never forget him," replied the sentinel, looking about him in a scared manner, as though he expected to find the person spoken of, close to his elbow, notwithstanding he had seen him go into the building, after Cromwell.

While the guard was thus, with anxious and dismayed looks, discussing what had happened, Cromwell preceded the grey man into the palace. Taking a key from his pocket, he with trembling hands unlocked a door that led to a long picture gallery. The grey man still followed, and when the gallery was traversed in its whole length, Cromwell by the aid of another key, opened a very small door, of a shape that belonged to the gothic style of architecture. They both passed in.—The door was closed, and then all was still.

*   *   *   *   *   *   *

In half an hour the grey man, with a calm step, passed out from St.

James's, but when Cromwell's secretary, a young man named Redgrave, sought him, he found him resting his head upon his hands, trembling violently. Redgrave had no wish to listen to anything his master might say unadvisedly—he knew well the danger of such a course, but as he involuntarily paused upon seeing Cromwell in such an unwonted state of agitation, he could not help hearing a few words that came from his lips.

"No! no! no!" he said, "not that—not that.—Let me die in some other form than that.—I have dreamt horrors enough.—Let not so hideous a reality dawn upon my soul.—No, no, no.—Come no more if you come with so fearful a prophetic greeting.—Oh, spare me—spare me!"

Redgrave would gladly have retreated, but he feared to move, lest by doing so he should attract the notice of Cromwell, who seeing him going might fancy he had only come to listen. He was, as it were, compelled therefore to hear more.

"There! there!" added Cromwell, "keep off the crowd, but most of all keep off that grim and gory phantom.—Off—off.—God, oh, God!"

"Sir," said Redgrave, for he was really getting alarmed, "sir! sir! will it please you to—"

Cromwell sprung to his feet, and darting forward he clutched the secretary by the throat as he cried,—

"Dissembling knave! Traitor! Is it thus you creep upon my privacy. Is it thus you listen to the voice of my inmost thoughts. Base caitiff, what death ought to be too harsh and cruel for such as thou art?"

"Sir, I—I. Oh, sir, you do me wrong."

"Wrong?"

"Yes, indeed, good sir. I did not listen to you."

"You—you did not?"

"In good faith, no."

"Then what heard you, without listening?"

"I heard you call upon the name of God."

"Well?"

"No more, as I'm a living man, sir. I came, I do admit, with undue haste into your presence, and found you at prayers."

"At prayers! Art sure of that."

"What else could you be thinking of, sir, with such a name upon your lips."

"Aye, what else," said Cromwell, as he walked to a seat, and flung himself into it. "What else, indeed should engage my private time, but prayer. You are a shrewd guesser, Redgrave, and I think you are faithful."

"I am, indeed, sir."

"Well, well. Let it pass, and you will forget that I questioned you somewhat sternly, and if you forget it not, you will at all events keep the knowledge to yourself. I would not that all the world should know even so much as you know, Redgrave."

"My lips are sealed, sir."

"Are they really so?"

"Indeed they are. I consider it to be part of my office to hear, to see, and to say nothing of all that I hear and see."

"Well said, Redgrave, you are on the way to advancement."

Cromwell rose and left the room. Redgrave looked after him, and shook his head.

"I would not change places with you, Noll," he said, "but I will soon I hope change my place, for it irks me sorely to play a part here, when my heart and inclinations run so differently. Now, if I were as great a rogue as I am a cavalier, and a lover of mine ease, and mine enjoyment, how easy it would be for me to rid the royal cause of such a stumbling block as Cromwell. But, no, I won't do it. While I do serve him I will serve him faithfully, and not all the world should tempt me to play him false; but I like not my service for all that, and if our merry England gets much more puritanical than it is, I must perforce leave it to get my jaws into the habit of laughing again, and yet I do think I shall leave even old Noll with regret. He has some good qualities, and at times I don't know whether I don't absolutely like him ; but, betray him, I never will. I'd rather say, God bless him ! than Die Cromwell ! and do the deed that should make my words prophetic."

A heavy hand was laid upon the secretary's shoulder. He turned hastily, and beheld Cromwell. Upon the stolid iron-looking countenance of Oliver, there were traces of unwonted emotion. A twitching movement about the mouth, and an unusual and for him most extraordinary moisture about the eyes, showed that he was strongly and strangely moved.

" Sir, sir !" stammered Redgrave.

" Yes," said Cromwell, " you deny playing the eaves-dropper upon me, but I have played it upon you, Redgrave."

" Then you have heard ——"

" Enough ——"

" To destroy me, and send me away disgraced."

" Or to cherish you, and keep you honoured."

Redgrave was silent, and after a slight pause, Cromwell continued—" You have spoken freely of me. Why do you not speak as freely to me. Do you think that I am one of those who detest plain honesty ? No, Redgrave, your censure is more musical, than much of the adulation that falls upon the ear of the victorious general, and—and so you think, Redgrave, if I were not a puritan—a commonwealth man, and a general against kingly state, you could almost say ' God bless me !' "

" You know my secret, sir."

" Secret ? What secret ?"

" That in my heart, I am a cavalier and royalist."

" Remain so Redgrave, so long as I know your other secret."

" Other secret, sir ?"

" Yes, that in addition to being a royalist you are an honest man. Oh, Redgrave, tell me that you wish the first Charles lived again, tell me that you wish to see the second of the name upon his ancestral throne ; but stay by me, Redgrave for you are honest."

" Can my idle speech have thus moved you, sir."

" Call it not idle. If between the rising and the setting of a sun, one heart full of true honour and nobility of sentiment and feeling be found, what a glorious day's work has been achieved. You will stay with me, Redgrave ?"

" I will sir."

" Thanks, thanks. You will be near to my heart. Redgrave, I am surrounded by false cringing knaves ; men who would full-mouthed like a hunting pack yelp me to the block. I know them, and I do not trust them. But you are an enemy, and I can trust you."

" Ah sir, if—if——"

" If what, Redgrave ?"

" If you would become the champion of a king, surrounded by such constitutional checks, that he dared not play the part of him who is gone——"

" Hush ! hush ! It cannot be. I have chosen my path, and must pursue it. No more—no more of that, but remember you are my friend, as well as my secretary, Redgrave."

" I accept the title, sir, with much joy."

Cromwell grasped him by the hand for a moment, and said—" Step, when you will, between me and my anger, and I will listen to you."

Without another word then he left the room, and Redgrave certainly felt that he had gone through one of the most important interviews, which he was ever likely to have with any living being.

" Confound it," he cried, as he strode from the room, and traversed the long picture gallery. " He will make me absolutely like him if I don't mind ; but let me remember. He gives me leave to step between him and his anger when I will. That is something. I may by staying here prove a sheet anchor to such of the king's party who may fall into the clutches of this, what shall I call him. Upon my faith he is a being of such contrarieties, that I can find no fitting word which shall describe him to the life. Yes, I will stay."

Redgrave felt that he could now stay in the service of Cromwell, into which, necessity had in the first instance driven him, with much more comfort and honour than he could before. In the first place he had no part to play which was obnoxious to his feelings, for Cromwell knew exactly who and what he was; and then again there was the pleasing feeling that he had an amount of interest with the most powerful and remarkable man of the age, which he might have the opportunity of exercising in the most beneficial way, for those who might by the chances of civil commotion fall into his, Cromwell's hands. Taking these views of the case, it need not be wondered at, that the more he, Redgrave, thought of the affair, the more pleased he was with the recent interview he had had with the great parliamentary general. Of the visit of the mysterious grey man he, Redgrave, just then knew nothing, but he was soon informed of it by an officer of the guard, whom he met, and he made no doubt in his own mind, but that the state of strange agitation in which he found Cromwell, was immediately subsequent to the interview with that most mysterious personage. He exhausted his mind with conjectures, as to who and what the grey man could possibly be, but he could form no hypothesis upon the subject, that bore about it anything of the aspect of probability. At length, having retired to his chamber, he fell asleep, full of strange thoughts, but to have strange dreams of forthcoming events, which his sagacity painted faintly to his imagination during his state of somnolency. As yet the bruit of the dissolution of the long parliament, was but slowly making its way throughout the metropolis. Oliver Cromwell passed the remainder of that night in earnest consultation with some of his officers, and it was settled that a new and more compliant parliament should be called together forthwith.

CHAPTER VI.

RETURNS TO CROFT'S CASTLE, AND THE LOVERS.

WE left young Courtney and Mary at the house of Walk-in-the-right-path Strangeways, in certainly rather an equivocal position. Perhaps, it would have been just as well if Cromwell had stayed a little longer, in order to curb the growing fury of the puritan, and place family matters if possible in a more agreeable and amiable condition, but the deep disappointment he felt at not capturing Charles II., in some measure incapacitated him from playing the part of a mentor or a peace maker. When the moral influence of his presence was no longer there to check Strangeways, he burst out into just such a torrent of wrath as such a religious man might be supposed to give way to, upon affairs not taking the exact turn which he hoped, wished, and looked forward to.

"Son of a malignant," he cried, addressing Charles Courtney, "how dare you show yourself in this house? Ought I not to take the life of the enemy of the Lord."

"Forbear, sir," said Charles. "There was a time, Master Strangeways, when as you well know, before you thought proper to become a puritan, and a follower of what you call the new light, you were not loath to receive me as the suitor of your daughter Mary, but now——"

"Away scoffer—away."

"Nay, sir, hear me out. 'Tis you who have changed, not I."

Strangeways looked savagely at Charles, who continued,—"Whether that change be a conscientious one, or one merely adopted for the purpose of gaining something by being in the fashion of the times, it is not my business, neither is it my inclination to enquire, but consequent upon that change you forbade me your house."

"Leave it now, man of Belial."

"Not until I have said all that I wish to say. Love, sir, may be for a time trodden down, but it never can be trodden out. I could not—I would not live without the joy of seeing and conversing with Mary, I did not see that I was called upon to do so merely because you had thought proper to adopt certain religious and political opinions."

"Charles! Charles!" said Mary.

She was fearful that in his indignation he was saying what would make an irreconcilable breach between him and her father.

"Nay, nay, Mary," he said, "fear nothing. Your father I will so far compliment as to believe he likes to hear the truth best, and I am telling it to him. His own heart tells him that each word that I am now uttering upon this painful occasion, bears upon it the full impress of verity."

Strangeways scowled at him, and Mary was silent.

"Feeling, then," continued Courtney, "that I could not live without seeing Mary, I was equally determined to see her as to see her with honour. So, sir, we are married, and I can really and truly present Lady Courtney to you, for I hold my rank."

"Rank!" cried Strangeways.

"Yes, sir, rank. Charles the Second has made me Sir Charles Courtney."

"When Charles the Second has a kingdom, it is time for him to make knights," said the puritan. Leave my house."

"Come, Mary."

"No, no!" roared Strangeways.

"Sir."

"Fancy you, malignant, that you are to come hither and steal my child. No. Never shall she cross my threshold in your company. Come hither, Mary, and remember to whom you owe your first duty."

"Bread and water," said Mrs. Strangeways; "a dark room, and prayer, shall be your portion, undutiful girl. Come with me."

"Madam," said Mary, "I have made a vow. In my calm judgment I have sworn to love, to honor, and to obey him whom my heart preferred to all the world beside. Charles, I am yours, and yours only."

She clung to the arm of the young cavalier, and he held her round the waist with his left hand, while his right strayed to the hilt of his sword, for he saw that there was menace and danger in the glance of Strangeways.

"Beware, sir," he said. "Heaven knows that for the sake of one who is dear to me, I would fain be well with you, but I am not of a temper to brook any serious wrong. So once again I say, sir, beware."

"My daughter is no wife!"

"Shame, shame upon you, Master Strangeways, to be the traducer of your own child's honour. I would make any one else but you who uttered such a base calumny eat their words at my sword's point. It is your duty, madam, to protect your daughter from slander."

"My duty," said Mrs. Strangeways, "is to walk in the way of the Lord."

"And mine," said Strangeways, suddenly presenting a pistol at Charles Courtney, "is to take revenge against the seducer of my child."

A shriek from Mary did not prevent the puritan from pulling the trigger, but the pistol only flashed in the pan. Charles was about to speak, but Mary interrupted him; for with an energy that no one would have thought her capable of exerting, she cried,—

"Father, you have now separated yourself from me for ever. Never again attempt to cross the ocean you have placed between us. Charles, come away— come away."

It was evident that Charles Courtney could not trust himself to speak, and he would have left the house in peace, even after this atrocious attempt upon his life, but Strangeways flew to one of the windows, and, flinging it open, cried in a loud voice,—

"A malignant! A malignant!"

This was a cry which in London at that time was always sufficient to get together a ferocious, ignorant, and fanatical mob, and this was just what the cold-blooded puritan wanted to do, for if he could have sacrificed poor Charles Courtney, it would have given him great delight.

"This way," whispered Charles to Mary. "To the boat."

Mr. Strangeways made a slight attempt to stop them, but the flash of the long bright rapier which Charles at the moment chanced to draw, somewhat bewildered his faculties.

"Let those who stay me," cried Courtney, "look to their own safety, for, by heaven, I will not now."

These words were spoken much too heartily, and accompanied by much too significant a wave of the long rapier, to be considered as at all idle ones, and no member of Walk-in-the-right-path Strangeway's household, although he called upon them to do so, thought proper to test in his own proper person the sincerity of the young cavalier's words.

"Oh, mother, mother!" cried Mary, "you will not part from me thus—you at least will give your child a blessing."

Mrs. Strangeways made no answer, but showed some symptoms of fainting; while Strangeways himself called still from the window into the low thoroughfare close at hand,

"A malignant—a malignant!"

Courtney half carried Mary into the garden, and then with his sword still in his hand, he strode onwards towards the little steps, where he had left his boat, and which, it was quite a mercy, had not been seen by Cromwell and his party.

"Oh, Charles, this is dreadful," said Mary.

"Courage, courage!"

"They would have murdered you."

"Which we will forgive, my Mary! since the attempt was a failure. We will never talk of that again."

"You are too—too good."

"The love of you, Mary, I think has made something of me. Do not weep —we shall be happy, very happy, dear one! despite all the clouds that now seem lowering over our fortunes. Fate will not always persecute us—come, cheer up!"

"I will strive to do so, Charles."

"And to strive is to do it. I am thinking anxiously where I may best bestow you for a time. Can you suggest aught?"

"Yes, Charles; if I could but get to the house of my old nurse, Bridget Lee, I should not only be safe but affectionately cared for."

"And where is she?"

"By Southwark. If we could land at a small quay, called King's Ferry, I could find the way."

"I know it well; come on, come on. My boat is no doubt in safety, for I moored it close in shore; and once in it, and upon the bosom of the Thames, I shall think we are safe and free. Come, courage now — courage! and fancy yourself indeed a cavalier's bride! Why, the day will come when you will laugh at this night's adventure, and both your father and mother, having grown wiser by seeing that you have grown happier, will shake hands with me yet!"

"And you so noble and so forgiving!" said Mary, as a gush of tears came to her relief. "Oh, Charles, Charles! why will you make me love you more and more, my own Charles!"

The boat was gained, and placing his young bride carefully in it, the cavalier pushed away from the land into the middle of the stream; but almost as he did so, he saw three boats, well manned, push out from a small quay close at hand, while not only persons on the shore, but persons likewise who were in the boats, shouted—

"A malignant—a malignant!"

"We are lost!" said Mary.

"Lost? Nay, Mary, not so."

"In five minutes they will be upon our track."

"Five minutes!" laughed Charles. "It is time enough to win a battle, and certainly more than time to win a boat race in."

In another moment the young cavalier was seated, and plying his oars with a strength and skill that sent the little lightly-laden boat at a tremendous pace through the water. The other boats, having many men in them, moved but slowly.

"Look up Mary," said Courtney, "and see what an unequal race this is. We have it all our own way."

"A malignant! a malignant!" again shouted the fanatics, who had been stirred up by Walk-in-the-right-path Strangeways.

But the pursuit of the cavalier by such means as were at the disposal of the mob would have been fruitless, but for the circumstance that an eight oared galley, which was upon the river, joined in the chace. A glance at the costume, and general appearance of the persons in the galley was quite sufficient to convince the cavalier, that they were no friends of the royal cause, and for the first time he felt that there was some danger. He redoubled his exertions, and Mary, who as she sat did not see the galley, could not for some few moments conceive, why he thought or found it necessary to make so much speed. A glance however in the direction where his eyes were fixed, let her see the danger.

"Charles, Charles, they will murder you. Oh, God help us now!"

"Hush, hush Mary. You will unnerve me. Hush. We are not lost yet. Believe me we are not lost yet."

"But there is much real danger."

"From which we will yet extract much real safety. Courage, courage. Courage my Mary."

"Give way!" cried a stern voice on board the eight oared galley, and the watermen, if they were such, bent to their oars with right good will, straining evidently every nerve to come up with the small boat. But still the little wherry with its light draught and two passengers merely, kept on gallantly, and at times it actually seemed to spring from the water, and bound on some yards like a living thing, under the impetus given to it by the young cavalier. Mary clasped her hands in prayer, and then pursued and pursuer both neared the old landing place at Whitefriars, where there seemed to be not a soul.

CHAPTER VII.

THE CAVALIER CLUB.—AN ALARM.

THAT eventful night has passed away, and another day-dawn is added to England's commonwealth. Far and near the report of the violent and unprecedented manner in which the parliament, with all its faults, had been dissolved, had caused much commotion, and in London there was almost an utter stagnation of all ordinary business, for all men's minds were full of alarm. Some predicted a civil war between the adherents of the long parliament, and those who might now be called the partisans of Oliver Cromwell, for by the act he had had the audacity to commit, he had quite in a manner of speaking, erected himself into a separate state. Others again were fairly of opinion, that he would seize the ruins of kingly power, and being wafted into the throne upon the breath of the army,

THE PURITAN ABOUT TO SHOOT THE CAVALIER FOR MARRYING HIS DAUGHTER

he would establish a rule at once vigorous and despotic. None of these supposition were true, although they all more or less contributed to produce confusion, and to unhinge society more particularly in the metropolis. That Cromwell had at this juncture great power, and that some about him urged him to aspire to the kingly state, there can be no doubt, but either his lack of ambition or sagacity pointed out a different course. Before twelve o'clock on the succeeding day, he announced the intention of immediately summoning a new parliament, whose servant he protested he would be, as he said he would have been the servant of the other, if it had been honest. Writs were issued for the election of members but it was well enough perceived, that if the returns did not please the dictator, the new commons would not be long without sharing the fate of the old. Cromwell was willing enough to be called a servant, always provided he had a tractable and obedient master. The disposition and concomitants of that new parliament which was called together by Oliver Cromwell after the dissolution by an act of unprece-dented violence of the long parliament, are tolerably well known. The new body was composed of men, many of whom were of good ability, but the majority was for a time entirely subservient to the will of Cromwell, as a military dictator. Among the body, too, were some who brought contempt upon it. But then we have at present some members of our own reformed House of Commons who are quite as contemptible as any of Cromwell's Commons could by any human possi-bility be. It is true we have not one now rejoicing in the name of Praise-God Barebones, as Cromwell had, but we have many who are quite as fanatical and quite as illiberal and contemptible as the leather-seller who occupied a seat in the parliament called by Cromwell. Our business, however, just now, is with a dif-ferent class of men, neither do we wish to anticipate the regular course of events. The day had just come to a close, when an individual attired in sad coloured gar-ments walked slowly down Abingdon-street, Westminster. His pace was an easy one, indeed. He almost seemed to be practising how short a distance he could go with the most show of walking. When he got to the end of the street he turned abruptly, and in the same manner traversed again its whole length. This parad-ing to and fro was kept up for a considerable period of time. Indeed, the solitary man had been upon his post for nearly an hour before he met with any interrup-tion. Then a man in a cloak, with a slouched hat, passed him, and as he did so he spoke, but without in the smallest degree pausing.

"Ravens or eagles?" he said.

"Eagles all," replied the man, who was evidently keeping watch for some pur-pose in Abingdon-street.

The new comer immediately ascended the steps of a large house, and rapidly ap-plying a key to the lock of the door, he opened it and went in, carefully closing it behind him. In succession twelve persons came in the same way, and after a simi-lar question and answer from the man in the street, made their way into the house. He still continued his monotonous walk, for his duty was not over, and while he is continuing it, we will follow the last comer into the large house for the sake of a complete introduction to the others. Immediately upon closing the door behind, this person listened attentively, and finding that there was no noise in the house, he made his way, dark as it was, with a degree of precision that showed he was well acquainted with the premises, towards a small room upon the ground floor of the house. This room was quite destitute of furniture, and in a very dirty and much dilapidated condition. There came just sufficient of the twilight which was without, through a dusky window, to enable any one to see his way about the room. The man made his way at once to the fire-place, where there seemed to be an ordinary grate. With his key he tapped thrice upon the iron back of the grate, and in a moment there came a similar sound faintly from the other side. He then turned the grate half round, for it was so constructed as to turn upon a centre, leaving upon each side of it room enough for a moderate sized man to creep through.

"It is you, Sir Walter Cardwell," cried a voice.

"Yes," said the person who had turned the grate. "I am late, I think."

"Better late than never," said another.

He crept through the narrow opening on one side of the grate, and having re-placed it in its original position, he was welcomed in a small but richly appointed room by the eleven others, who had all preceded him by the same rather singular mode of entrance. The apartment was without any window to it, indeed it more resembled a cupboard ingeniously contrived in the architecture of the house, than a room. There was not much more room than enough to hold the twelve men, and allow them to move about a little, without absolutely running against each other. A thick and uncommonly handsome carpet, that completely deadened all sound of feet, was upon the floor, and the walls were hung completely round with the same material, so that even a loud voice could scarcely have made itself heard, beyond the precincts of that room. A round table covered with velvet, stood in the centre of the little apartment, and close to it the chairs, which were for the use of the persons who were there assembled. In one corner were several of the short, thick, clumsy looking carbines of the period, and some highly finished, and richly mounted swords, were likewise in the room. The company were all well, but plainly dressed.

"Will you preside, Sir Walter?" said one.

"Nay, there are worthier!"

"Not a whit! Not a whit!"

"Well, gentlemen, if it be your pleasure, I will not waste precious moments in idle scruples. God save the king!"

"Amen!" said everybody.

Sir Walter Cardwell had taken his place in a chair with arms to it, and the others, with one exception, had grouped themselves round the table. That one sat apart, close to one particular portion of the wall, where a piece of the thick carpeting was cut, so as just to show the end of a metal whispering tube, which no doubt communicated with some one who kept special watch over the safety, and the solitude of the house, next door, which was made the thoroughfare by which the members of the Cavalier Club sought this place of meeting.

"All clear," said a strange faint voice, through the tube.

"Alls right, gentlemen," said he who had his post at it, "commence proceedings. I think once again, we have outwitted the crop eared knaves."

"Well, gentlemen," said Sir Walter Cardwell, "here we are all good men, and true, and liege subjects of King Charles the Second. This plan of ours of having so many different places of meeting, is I really think the one of all others which will ensure our safety."

"Not a doubt of it," said another, "We have now at different parts of London, twelve such rooms as this, got at by various channels, so that meeting as we do regularly twice a week, we never excite continued attention in any one locality, to which we owe our safety."

"And when we hold a special mesting, as now." said Sir Walter, "we can fix upon any place which is most convenient. Has any member a report to make to the club."

"Yes. But will he be here to-night?"

"Doubtful. The king is at Sir William Davenant's, I think."

"Hush! I sometimes think even walls may have ears. Have you anything to tell us, my Lord Wilton."

"Little enough. Redgrave has been tried."

"Ah! and with success."

"No. The fellow won't move. He has some romantic notions of being faithful to Cromwell, and it is impossible to move him."

"Now really, how can a cavalier and a gentleman be so absurd. Since the murder of the king, we have decided that the enemy is not entitled to honourable treatment, but that anything is justifiable, that in any way will conduce towards the end we have in view."

"Of course," said several.

"And so you think that nothing at all can be made of Redgrave?"

"Certain. He said that he had better remain secretary to Cromwell, where he might do some good legitimately, but that while he retained his post, he would not betray Oliver, or Noll, as he called him."

"A romantic fool. Did you tell him that a baronetcy would be guaranteed to him, if he would transmit copies of all private papers that come through his hands, to the Hague."

"Yes, and that a seat in the lords would assuredly be his, if Cromwell was found dead in his private closet."

"What said he?"

"Why that he had heard there were bravoes in Venice, but hoped there were none in London."

"The fool!"

"Worse than fool. I do believe the fellow by living in a puritanical atmosphere is half a puritan himself now. But be that as it may, I am quite convinced that nothing can be done with him for our cause."

"Well, drop him.—And now Cromwell still lives, although Ralph Goddard had his commission, and part of his money. Has any one news of him?"

"Yes," said one, "I can tell you news of Goddard."

"Ah, indeed!"

"He was picked up dead to-day from the Thames, near Blackfriars, with his face completely smashed, and the hilt of a poignard so tightly clutched in his dead fingers that no one could get it away from him."

"Then he has failed."

"Unquestionably, for Cromwell lives, and as usual keeps the attempt upon his life a most profound secret."

"The politic knave!"

"We never questioned his talent"

"Well gentlemen," said Sir Walter Cardwell. "What are we to do now. I think my Lord Sefton, you had something to propose."

"I was wishing to say," began Lord Sifton, "that I think each day places us in a worse position.—What I want, is, that we should determine upon striking some blow for this unhappy country."

"But how?"

"Why thus. We know from our list that we can muster some seven hundred men in London, who at any given hour will act for us. Now what I propose, is, that those be divided into seven distinct divisions, at different parts of the town, and that at a certain hour they sally out headed by one of us, crying:—'Long live King Charles!' One of the hundreds can attack the palace, and I would have that hundred by all means, attired like Cromwell's troopers."

"Think you that would do?"

"I am of opinion that we should be joined by all the disaffected, troublesome, idle, bad characters in the metropolis, and so in a few hours, we might have a formidable force in London. I would then at a given signal, concentrate our power at Charing Cross, and make a bold attempt to overthrow the present state of things and proclaim the king."

"It might do."

"What disposable force has Cromwell in London?"

"Not now more than nine thousand men, since he sent so large a evy to Northumberland, and we have reason to believe, that the sixth infantry are wavering—small slips of paper have been industriously distributed among the troops, stating that when the king shall one day appear in London, fifty pounds and a free pardon, will be given to every man who joins his standard, and to the first hundred with arms in their hands, ten thousand pounds among them."

"With what effect?"

"That there is no means of knowing, but human nature is fond of advantages, and we may fairly reckon upon some of the men."

"Then what force do you calculate upon, my lord?"

"Why we start with seven hundred well-armed men, and I think we ought to expect seven hundred of the troops, to join us, and about enough rabble to make up three or four thousand men in all. Then if Cromwell be disposed of——"

"Aye!"

"Aye!—Aye!"

"Well, gentlemen, I suppose he is mortal?"

"Yes, but hitherto how he has baffled us all.—Oh, if Redgrave was but really and truly one of us, and would strike the necessary blow simultaneously with rising, then indeed we might count upon our power, but Cromwell is a host."

" He is indeed."

" Well, but we are not to lie quietly and submit, because Cromwell happens to be powerful, and his secretary crotchetty ?"

" Oh, certainly not. There is however, one important element in the whole affair, which may make us or mar us. Will the king head the movement, or will he not ?"

" I should," said Lord Sefton, " advise his majesty to be somewhat handy, so that we might call upon him to shew himself, in the event of our meeting with sufficient success' to make such a step desirable. He can be in the house of one of our friends, nobly attired and accoutred for the occasion."

" Well that might answer," said Sir Walter. " Will each of you gentlemen give this matter your most anxious and serious consideration, between now and our next night of meeting, and then we will endeavour to come to some conclusion upon it. I for one am favourable to it."

" And I," said another. " It has a character of boldness about it, which is to me enchanting as well as promising. Where do we meet on Friday ?"

" At the house in the fields by Isledon."

At this moment, he whose duty it was upon that night to remain by the tube, which would convey a whisper from some other sentinel, sprung to his feet crying—

" Danger !"

In an instant all rose, and Sir Walter holding up his hand said—" Silence gentlemen, cavaliers silence. Everything is to be done by silence and caution—nothing by tumult. What is the danger, Everend ?'

" A force, consisting of dismounted cavalry is in the street."

" Then we are betrayed !"

" Stop ! we are all here."

" Yes, but there may be a Judas !"

" Without, but not within," said Lord Sefton, " We all know each other too well, and we are too much committed to the royal cause, both in person and pocket to betray it. The treason is without, I suspect Adams."

CHAPTER VIII.

THE ALARM.—THE TRAITOR AND HIS FATE.

SOME confusion now ensued among the cavaliers. Adams was the name of the man who kept watch in the street without. He was a personal servant of Sir Walter Cardwell's.

" Stop !" said Sir Walter. " You suspect Adams, my lord. Pray tell me why ?"

" Simply because suspicion passes all here, and can only alight upon him. There is Waller, who has just told me in a voice of alarm through the tube, that the troopers of Cromwell are at hand, he and Adams are the only persons besides ourselves, who know we are here."

" Then we are lost," cried one."

" Let us die bravely, gentlemen," said another, as he drew his sword.

" We shall be all murdered," said a third, " but we will drag some of those puritanical scoundrels by the ears to the other world with us."

" Gentlemen, gentlemen ! hear me," said Sir Walter.

All was silent.

" How much does Adams know ?"

" Everything I suppose," said Lord Wilton.

" Pardon me, I never confide to a subordinate, more than is absolutely necessary for my own purpose, as well as to make him think he is trusted. Mind you I am not yet convinced of the treachery of Adams, but if it be a verity, the extent of his knowledge does not reach this room."

"Indeed !"

"He knows only that with keys, twelve gentlemen enter the house next door, but that we got here by the revolving grate, unless he be a conjuror, he knows nothing of."

"That's a mercy."

"We are much beholden to your prudence, Sir Walter.

"We cannot be too prudent. What does Waller say ?"

All were anxious to hear the report from the whispering tube, and Lord Sefton who had taken a station there, commenced a brief conversation with the man who was at the other end of it.

"Waller ! Waller !"

"I am here ?"

"What see you, now ?"

"The dismounted troops have halted in the street, and they are placing sentinels at different points. There seems to be some confusion."

"Where is Adams ?"

"I do not see him at all."

"Look carefully, Waller. We want most particularly to know if Adams be a prisoner, or in conversation confidentially with the enemy."

"There is a little throng of persons round a mounted officer, but the street has got so dark I can hardly distinguish the one from the other as yet. I can see nothing of Adams."

"Do you know the mounted officer ?"

"Yes, it is a Captain Latchford, in great esteem with Cromwell."

"Confound him !"

"Stop—now I see Adams."

"Where is he ?"

"Talking to Latchford, and leaning on the saddle, and patting the horse as he does so. They seem old friends."

"The villain !"

"Now they both laugh."

"Adams shall laugh a different sort of laugh to-morrow, if we escape this danger. Look to yourself, Waller, and destroy any indication of this tube on your side of the wall."

"Oh, never mind me. Hark! the troopers are marching towards the empty house. Be careful for Heaven's sake."

"We will—we will. God bless you, Waller."

The cavaliers awaited now in intense stillness the progress of events. They could not but feel that their safest course was to remain where they were, but then what an anxious and painful thing it was to do so. They looked at each other trying to read hope, when in some cases there was most certainly no such feeling present. It was a strange thing to note the different effects which the desperation of the circumstances in which they were placed, had upon the different individuals present. They all knew that death would be the result of discovery, and each man according to his habits and feelings, awaited the possibility, or we may almost say the probability of such a castrophe taking place within the next five minutes. Some sat looking calm and still, with their eyes nearly shut. Others again had a flush of increased colour upon their countenances, while some clenched their drawn swords, and by their compressed teeth, showed that they had a determination to die bravely. Sir Walter Cardwell sat in his presidential chair, looking, perhaps, the calmest of any, the only movement he made was one of caution now and then, by raising his hand, if any of his companions chanced to make some slight noise in shifting his position. Lord Sefton bent forward and whispered to him,—"It is quite dark in the next room. Some ray of light may make its way through a crevice."

"Right," said Sir Walter Cardwell.

On the instant then he extinguished the only light that they had burning in the room. There being no window, the most intense darkness now was in the place, no one could see his own hand if held up within six inches of his face. Not one of the number made any remark or any opposition to the extinguishing the light, for all seemed at once to comprehend the reason of it. It was an obvious measure of precaution. A few moments more, and the measured tramp of armed men came upon their ears. They heard the word to "halt!" given, and then some commands were issued in a tone which they did not catch, but they were aware that a body of troopers had halted at the door of the empty house. The ceremony of knocking, it was evidently considered would be quite a waste of time, and some blows from the brass bound stocks of the trooper's carbines soon burst the door open.

"Look out," said Adams. "They are desperate men."

"Oh we are used to such," replied Captain Latchford, as he dismounted; and giving his horse in charge to one of the soldiers, he entered the house.

Adams evidently hesitated as to what he should do. At one moment he seemed to think that his safest plan would be to go into the house along with the troopers, while at another he thought he had better stay where he was. Captain Latchford, however, decided the question by calling out to him in a loud tone,—

"Adams you are better here."

The traitor was just one of those men who will take a command from anybody at a moment, and now he rushed into the house, for he thought that if he were to go there he had better not be last. For all he knew, some of the cavaliers might from some room or another pounce upon him and take his life. His grand object now, therefore, was to get into the centre of the assailing force.

"You seem nervous," said Latchford.

"Oh not at all. Not at all."

A party of five troopers were left at the door step, with orders to shoot at once, without question or remark, any stranger who might try to leave the house, and there they waited with their carbines at full cock, so that certain death must have been the portion of any one trying to escape.

"I think," remarked Latchford, as his iron clad heels resounded through the passage, "that we have them now. The house is well-guarded, both back and front, and not a mouse can leave it now, unseen by my men."

"Yes," said Adams nervously. "Yes, you certainly have them now."

"And you will have the consolation of having done the state some service, Adams."

"Yes—yes—oh yes."

The party of troopers that entered the house consisted of twenty-five men, and now commenced a regular examination of room after room, the precaution being taken of placing a couple of sentinels at the door of every apartment that had been looked into and found empty. By this means Captain Latchford calculated upon being able to thoroughly hunt the house through, without allowing a possibility of the escape, by any secret passages, of the conspirators. A feeling both of surprise and vexation however, began soon to shew itself in the face of Latchford, as room after room was searched, without any one of them presenting the smallest indications of the presence of any one recently. The house was large, but by no means a complicated one as regarded its architecture, so that by the time the troopers had been over it, and two had been left at every door, Captain Latchford and Adams found themselves in the passage again, no wiser than they were.

"This is odd," said Latchford.

"Very," said Adams.

"Are you sure of the house?"

"Am I sure my head is upon my shoulders?"

"Well,—well."

"Besides, next door is in the occupation of Mr. Waller, a staunch puritan, and favourer of the new order of things, and upon the other side is the office for conducting some of the general's state affairs."

Latchford looked puzzled, and with a knowing sort of nod Adams said,—

"We have not been down-stairs."

"Well, let's go, in Heaven's name, and unearth the malignants, if we can. But I own I have doubts."

"Doubts of what?"

"Of anybody being here."

"Then I am mad, and see visions; for I counted twelve men go in at the street-door of this house, and I have not counted one come out."

"Then there is some most incomprehensible mystery in the whole affair, which, at present, is beyond our ken. Come on. We will not allow the lower regions of this house to escape our closest scrunity."

The officer and Adams, accompanied by the remaining troopers, made their way into the lower portion of the house, and then instituted so close a search, that it would have been quite impossible for anybody to have escaped them. In fine, they were quite convinced that no one was there.

"Now, Master Adams," said the captain, with some degree of asperity in his tone, "what do you say to all this?"

"Only one thing."

"And what may that be?"

"Why, that these cavaliers have, after all, given me but a half confidence, and that they have some hiding-place, that as yet I know nothing of."

"Well, that is a reasonable enough supposition."

"It is the only one I can think of. What will you do? Your judgment in such a matter as this is better than mine."

"I shall hold, for the present, military possession of the house."

"That will be well."

"I shall have a guard here, and then report the affair to the general. Perhaps he, with his wonderful sagacity in such matters, may be able to give some more satisfactory solution of the mystery than we can."

"It is probable."

The officer ordered the bugle to be faintly sounded in the passage, so as to recall all his sentinels at the different room doors, and then he picked out twelve men of his force, and left them in the house, under the orders of an officer of inferior rank, who was with the party.

CHAPTER IX.

THE ESCAPE OF COURTNEY AND MARY.

WE left Courtney, the young cavalier, and his beautiful bride, Mary, in a very critical and dangerous situation. The race that was now taking place between his wherry, only rowed by himself, and the eight-oared galley, was certainly a most unequal one. The only chance he now had of escape was in the probability, that although the galley gained upon him each instant, it might not actually reach him before he succeeded in gaining some comparatively safe landing place. Each fleeting moment, however, made this hope a more vain one, and it was with feelings akin to despair that the young cavalier saw the galley rapidly gaining on him. At the same time, the dusky forms of people on the shore, carrying lights of various descriptions, could be seen, while the shouts of impatience from their vindictive throats came clearly upon the night, or rather, the early morning. air.

"A malignant! Kill him! Slay him! Down with the malignant! Take his life! A malignant—a malignant!"

"You hear those bigots?" said Courtney.

"Oh, yes—yes, Charles.   They will kill you."

"Not yet, Mary.   Not yet."

Courtney now made almost superhuman efforts to distance the galley, and to run in to a small landing place that was near the Temple, but a very few minutes sufficed to convince him that it could not be done, and that very shortly the galley must overtake him.   He saw one of the men actually getting ready a long boat-hook for the purpose of catching the wherry.   With a sigh, he relaxed his endeavours to distance his pursuers, by rowing, for a few moments.   Taking from his pocket a pistol with a long bright barrel, he said to Mary,—

"Dids't ever, my darling, fire a pistol?"

"Oh, yes—yes."

"Then take this, and fire among the rowers of the galley. It may still give us a chance of escape."

"I cannot only fire a pistol, but for sport, my good kind cousin Stephen taught me to load one. Oh, yes—yes, Charles, I can defend you."

"There then is hope, my darling, for us. The pistol is already loaded with three bullets, and there is a powder flask containing both powder and ball. Crouch down as low as you can in the boat, and fire away at the rascals. I will pull away as hard as I can, and we may save ourselves yet."

Mary shuddered as she almost lay down in the boat, and presented the pistol.

"Now—now!" said Courtney. "Fire among them."

Bang! went the pistol.

'Hilloa!" cried Courtney. "You have sent some unwelcome visitors among them, Mary. See—they pause, and we are gaining upon them rapidly."

It was evident that the pistol shot had produced some confusion on board the galley, for the rowers nearly all ceased, and it was only now and then that an oar broke the surface of the stream with spray. In another moment a loud hoarse voice cried—

"Give way—give way!"

The galley again sped on, but watching it narrowly as Courtney was, he could now see that there were but six rowers at work. Mary's face was of a death-like paleness, and her lips were compressed She had evidently worked herself up to a pitch of desperation. She felt that she was called upon to defend what was the dearest object to her in all the world, and she so far, under the impulse of that one master-feeling, got rid of previously acquired feelings and prejudices. Her hands did not even tremble as she again rapidly loaded the pistol.—She was far past ordinary agitation, and she kept her eyes fixed upon the advancing boat most intently. It would seem now, that either the fanatics on the shore had given up all thoughts of capturing the Malignant, as they called poor Courtney, or that they were too intent upon watching the struggle between the wherry and the galley, to make any further disturbance, for all was still. It was evident that all the interest of the affair had concentrated itself upon the two boats. Just as Mary had got the pistol loaded again, Courtney cried to her,—

"Stoop, Mary, stoop! for the love of Heaven, stoop."

She shrunk down in the boat.

A flash of light came from the side of the galley, and then a loud report.—It was evident some fire-arm of much longer calibre than a pistol had been fired. With a sharp whistle, something flew close by the eyes of Courtney, creating a momentary confusion of intellect, but it was only for a moment.

"All's right, Mary," he cried. "Fire where you saw that flash come from."

Bang! went the pistol again, and this time a sharp clear cry of pain mingled with the echoes of its discharge.

"My brave girl," cried Courtney, "you have hit the rascal. Bravo!—bravo! One of them is in the water.—Bravo!"

Mary looked on intently.—A man from the galley had fallen into the river, and it was evident that the whole exertions of the crew were directed to get him into the galley again. Under such circumstances the galley only drifted with the stream, and each moment's delay was most precious to Courtney, for, animated now by the hope of an escape, he pulled away with a speed that was perfectly tremendous.

"Load—load, my girl," he cried. "Give them no peace. Never let an enemy alone when he is in confusion.—Load and fire!"

Rapidly Mary again commenced loading the pistol, and Courtenay suddenly shipping one of his oars, gave the boat such a twist with the other, that he completely altered his position in the water with the rapidity of thought. The object of this manœuvre was at first not apparent to Mary, and she feared that something had gone amiss. It was only, though, for one moment that she could be in any sort of doubt upon the subject, for the loud report of the carbine from the galley again awakened echoes far and near, and no doubt the shot with which it seemed to have been pretty well crammed, scattered over the spot so recently occupied by the wherry.

"Another miss," cried Courtenay, as he bent to the oars again, and made the little boat fly through the water. It takes them some time to fire and load that machine. Give it them again, Mary."

Mary could not speak, she felt as though she should be choked were she to attempt to utter a word. All she was aware of was, that never in her wildest dreams had she pourtrayed to herself such a source of horror and danger as that to which she was now, with her heart's best treasure, exposed, and all she seemed to hear was that he wished her again to fire at the galley. Another moment and the pistol was loaded. It happened though that the people of the galley had just got hold of their comrade who had fallen into the water, and were dragging him into the galley. Mary paused.

"Why do you not fire?" said Courtney

She made a prodigious effort, and managed to summon breath enough to reply to him.

"Wait—wait—wait——"

"For what?"

Now that she had spoken once the spell that had held her in thraldom seemed to be broken.

"Soon, Charles," she said, "soon. Do you not see how fast the sweet morning light is creeping on?"

"Yes; but——"

"Nay, nay—I can see all in the galley clearly: a man is busily loading a carbine. Trust to me, Charles, and row on—he shall not fire it."

Mary now laid the barrel of the pistol upon the side of the boat, and looked along it with a wary eye.

"Can you really fire truly?" said Courtney.

"I can—I can."

"And are you calm enough?"

"Quite, Charles, quite; feel my hand."

"'Tis very cold."

"My heart feels cold too, Charles; but I am very calm. Row on. Oh, do not pause a moment now. There now, I see him—he has loaded the carbine and comes forward—he stoops. The morning light shines upon his face!"

Mary fired; and Courtney, whose eyes had likewise been fixed upon a man in the galley who had a carbine in his hand, saw him fall backwards among his companions, and the carbine was discharged in the air.

"You have hit him!" said Charles, "by Heaven, Mary, you have hit him!"

"For you, Charles! On—on—on!"

Charles needed now no one to stimulate him to exertion. The prospect that there was of present escape was quite sufficient to do so. But now it was quite clear that no accident, except to the actual rowers on board the galley, would induce them to pause again. They began to see how much time they had lost by pausing at every shot they received from the wherry, and they came now dashing on at a good pace. The landing-place was close at hand, where Charles wished to run in his wherry, and he made for it in a direct line.

But what was his agony at the moment when he thought that success was his, and escape was almost within his actual grasp, to see a large boat push off, in which there were some half dozen men, each with long horsemen's pistols in their hands. This boat was only rowed by two men, but they evidently had a perfect and accurate knowledge of what they were about; and it shot out into the stream with great ease and rapidity.

"Lost!" said Charles.

"Oh, God help us!" said Mary.

A shout of exultation burst from the people on board the galley. Mary's pistol was unloaded, and all Charles Courtney could now do, was to ship his oars and draw his sword, awaiting the struggle that he thought now inevitable.

The boat that had just left the landing-place steered close by him.

"Keep off, as you value your lives!" cried Courtney.

"Pho! pho! Sir Charles," said a voice, "have you changed sides, and are you going to turn traitor!"

"Good God!"

"Hush!"

"What is it—what is it?" cried Mary.

Charles Courtney sunk back in his boat, and gasped—

"The King!"

"Hurrah! hurrah!" cried the people on board the galley, for to all appearance, as they were situated, it seemed as if the boat that had put off from the landing-place had taken Charles Courtney prisoner. They soon found out their mistake.

"Odds fish, my lords, give them a volley," said a voice.

The pistols were simultaneously discharged at the galley. For about half a minute the cloud of smoke from the fire-arms obscured all objects; but when a puff of wind suddenly blew it aside, as though a curtain had been withdrawn, the effect of the volley was quite apparent in a most startling manner. The galley was drifting with the current merely—most of the oars were floating in the water, and the greatest confusion was evidently on board of her. Her crew and company seemed to be tumbling over each other, and there was all the appearance of a general fight amongst them.

"Bravo!" said the same voice that had given him orders to fire. "Bravo! a well directed discharge that! completely deserved by a set of scoundrels that would fire upon a young girl. The crop-eared knaves! Odds fish—I never suffered so much yet as I have in rage and impatience for the last half hour."

"Load your pistols," cried another. The vagabonds are recovering from the temporary confusion."

The tumult on board the galley had certainly ceased, and some of the oars were moved from the water, and again placed in the rollocks. A moment's observation of the persons in the galley showed that they had had quite enough of the affair, for, instead of making the least attempt to follow the boat, they sheered off. As if to deprecate the idea of another discharge of fire arms at them, one of them hoisted a white handkerchief at the end of an oar.

"A flag of truce!" said Courtney.

"Odds fish, we are masters of the Thames, at all events," said the same voice that had given the command to fire. "Come, Sir Charles, your safest plan will be to take refuge with us. We are going across the water to Dickinson's, and then to the Dutchman."

"Your majesty has saved me," said Courtney.

"Tush, man, tush—we all keep on saving each other."

"Is that the king?" whispered Mary.

"Yes, dear, that is Charles the Second."

Charles himself stood up, and helped Mary into the larger boat, saying as he did so,—

"Your gallantry this day shall not be forgotten; we must institute some military order in which to enrol those ladies who show what true British blood flows in their veins. By what name shall I have the pleasure to remember one who is as fair as she is brave?"

"Lady Courtney is much beholden to your majesty," said Courtney, placing a marked emphasis on the word lady."

"Lady Courtney?" said King Charles.

"Yes, your majesty."

"Odds fish, have you had time to get married? Are the parsons on the Thames, Sir Charles, eh?"

"No, sire, but there are clergymen of the true sort yet in London, and, some seven weeks since, Lady Courtney and I availed ourselves of the service of one."

"Indeed."

"It is so, sire—she is now flying with me from her father's house because he does not exactly wish me for a son-in-law."

"A Puritan?"

"Yes, sire."

"Well, Courtney, we are getting on surely, for if we take from the Puritans all their fairest maidens we shall leave them poor indeed. Lady Courtney, we will hope that the day is not far distant when we shall have a court and a queen to entertain you."

Mary bowed, for there was a something about the tone and manner of Charles which did not induce her to enter into conversation with him. She could not help, though, in her heart admiring one feature in his character, and that was his betraying no suspicion of her, although Courtney had told him that she was the daughter of a Puritan. There was not the smallest cloud of doubt upon his face, nor the least stray expression of any idea that she could betray him. This might have been heroism on the part of Charles the Second, or it might have been that kind of reckless constitutional carelessness, of which during his adventurous career he gave so many proofs; at all events it was pleasing, and upon many occasions it had the effect of gaining him friends when a show of suspicion would have made him enemies. Courtney let the little wherry go with the stream, for now that he and Mary had taken refuge in the larger boat, it was no longer desirable to be encumbered by its presence.

CHAPTER X.

THE DANGER OF THE CAVALIERS.—AN AFFRAY.

WE leave Courtney and his fair young bride in high company; for not only did the large boat contain Charles the Second himself, but there was likewise with him some of the most influential and well known noblemen who were attached to the royal cause. This was one of those junctures at which, just before the full power of Oliver Cromwell was as consolidated as it afterwards became, the cavaliers thought there was a chance by a popular commotion of recovering back the mass of the people to royalty. The royal party could never persuade itself that the love of kingly institutions was extinct in the minds of the English people; and that they were quite right in that opinion was abundantly manifested by the slavish adulation with which a licentious tyrant was eventually welcomed to the throne after the death of Cromwell, and the deposition of his weak and imbecile son Richard, who proved to the world that talent and energy are by no means hereditary gifts. Hence continual futile attempts were made by the royalists to fan into a flame this slumbering loyal, kingly feeling, that they fancied lay slumbering in the houses of the English people. That these attempts neither retarded nor accelerated the Restoration is evident enough. The mass of the people have no political opinion at all, and they just follow the course of events. An abounding and all-engrossing selfishness is the grand characteristic of the middle classes of society in England. That is the leading star of all their actions; and their attachment to a court, and to courtly institutions, merely consists in the fact that there is so much plunder consequent upon its institutes, that each man lives in hope of coming in for some special share of it. A tradesman in Oxford-street or Regent-street cares about as much for national freedom and national economy as he does for the statistics of Tartary, always provided he gets his share of the plundered wealth of the people by pampering by his wares the lavish extravagance of a depraved court. The secret of the popular support which is given to such

Governments as our own, and such State Churches, lies simply in the fact, that a great mass of the people is bribed by the money stolen from the whole; and those who do not come in for a share of the State plunder feel like folks who have got a blank in a lottery—still a hankering not to destroy the wheel, but to have another draw. The people who cheered Charles the Second upon his entry into London, to assume the kingly state, would just as readily have shouted at his execution. But to our story.

We will leave Sir Charles Courtney—Mary—the king, and the boatful of nobility, to pursue their way to the house of a staunch royalist, named Dickinson, on the Surrey side of the water, and where there was ample shelter and accommodation for all, while we take another glance at the critical situation of the twelve cavaliers who were shut up in the small room in Abingdon-street, Westminster. Of course, their great hope and expectation was, that, after searching the house and finding them not there, the troopers would be withdrawn, and that after a time given to caution, they, the cavaliers, could quietly emerge. The tactics of the captain of the little band which was charged by Cromwell with this duty, however, altered all that. In the most annoying manner, it will be recollected, he had left a dozen well-armed men and an officer on the premises. And what made the dilemma worse was, that there was no opening from the little room into the house of Waller next door, and even if there had been such, it would scarcely have been safe to have left by his house-door, for it was more than probable that some sentinels were left in the street to keep a strict watch upon all that took place. To be sure a short time might have sufficed to break down a sufficient portion of the wall to make an entrance into Waller's house; but it was very questionable whether the noise consequent upon such an operation would not be heard in the empty house. In that case, an alarm would be given, and their destruction would be the certain and immediate result of it.

Truly a more painful position they thought they could scarcely be in, for they heard quite distinctly the orders given for the twelve men to remain, and the fact that they did so was ample warning to them not to indulge in any conversation, lest with equal facility their voices should reach the ears of the troopers; patience was all they had left them to fall back upon. Then they were in the dark, and each moment appeared to them a whole day of anxiety and apprehension. It is true that when, from no one interfering with the grate, they felt sure that Adams had not divined the secret of their hiding place, they felt a little easier, but still the next few hours must be to them of vital importance, for food they had none. They heard the troopers tramping about the house, and slamming doors violently to. Then they heard some heavy work going on, as though the soldiers were intent upon destroying the house, but they were soon made aware of what was the object of the blows they heard struck and the crashing of timber. A tramping of feet took place in the room adjoining.

"This seems the largest," said a voice; "one of these doors laid along on these bricks, we have found will make a seat for us all."

"Ay, will it," said another.

"Less noise!" said an authoritative voice.

From the effect which this had upon the men, the cavaliers guessed that the officer had spoken; they were much more quiet now, and only the knocking about of the door that they had broken from its hinges to make a seat of was heard. To the intense annoyance and agony of the cavaliers, it was clear that the troopers, by some fatal accident, had chosen that room from all the others as the one in which to remain. Then all hope of escape for some time seemed to be quite extinguished, unless some extraordinary accident should happen of a favourable nature to the cavaliers, who were in the little room. That did not seem highly probable. Sir Walter Cardwell ventured, in a whisper, to speak to Lord Wilton.

"What can we do?" he said,—

"I know not," was the reply. "We are in such desperate straits, that our only chance is to watch what is going on, and take advantage of any opportunity that may arise for bettering our most desperate condition."

"Hush! be cautious."

"I am so."

"Yes; but I mean as you go on speaking you are apt to raise your voice. Remember what a trifle would betray us to certain death."

"That is true."

"There is one thing that we are pretty well aware of, gentlemen," said he who happened to be the nearest to Sir Walter Cardwell and Lord Wilton, and so heard what they said, "there is one thing that we are perfectly aware of, and that is, that our situation, short of absolute capture, cannot be worse than it is."

At this precise moment, as though some malignant destiny had taken a pleasure in striking from under them the smallest spot upon which hope could rest, one of the soldiers said aloud,—

"It's cold here, and damp. Has any one the means of lighting a fire. There's a grate all ready."

"Good—good!" ejaculated Sir Walter Cardwell.

"It would be more comfortable," said another trooper, "than sitting staring at each other in the cold, at all events."

"Oh, ye wretches!" said a third, in a conventicle tone; "oh, ye wretches!"

"What's the matter with you!" said the first speaker.

"Ye are more intent upon what you call your comforts, than in praising the Lord, which you ought to do always. I propose a psalm."

"Well, but surely we may have both the psalm and the fire. I dare say a little gunpowder will soon light it, and we can tear down paper from the walls. Here goes to make us comfortable, for who knows but we may have to stay here all night."

"I'm sure we shall," said another, ' for I heard the captain give orders to a file of men to go to the guard-house by the Bird-cage-walk, and bring us some refreshment as soon as might be."

"Did you so?"

"In truth did I."

"Very well, then we shall enjoy it as well again with a fire, and we will get another door down, and make a table of it."

"Well, there's no situation," said another, "but it may be made worse or better, as folks like themselves."

"Do you hear?" whispered Sir Walter Cardwell to Lord Wilton

"I do indeed."

"What is to be done?"

"God knows."

"Are we to wait here, and be smoked to death like bees in a hive, or wasps in an orchard?" said Sir James Manning.

A general hush was the reply to him, for in the excitement of the moment he had spoken in rather too high a tone, much higher indeed, than, under the circumstances, was at all warranted by prudence. But he was rather a reckless man, his courage ever degenerating into indiscretion.

"Perhaps they will fail after all in lighting a fire," said Lord Sefton.

Sir Walter Cardwell shook his head, as he replied,—

"Soldiers seldom fail in those sort of manœuvres. If they have made up their minds to have a fire, a fire they will have, you may depend upon it, by some means or another."

Sir Walter's opinion of Cromwell's troopers was well enough, as it appeared, founded. In the course of a few moments more, a large sheet of paper was torn from the wall, and crammed into the grate with some gunpowder wrapped up in it. Then with a sword a part of the door was cut down, and piled upon it as closely as possible, while a quantity more was got ready to feed the flame when it should arise.

"We shall be too safe," said Sir Walter Cardwell, with a faint smile.

"How mean you?"

"Why, no one will touch the grate when it is red hot, which in all probability it will soon be, now."

"The safety of death."

"No, gentlemen. We are, after all, twelve cavaliers to twelve troopers, and an officer. If we find our position quite untenable, we can and will fight our way out of it. But that should be a last resource, for our lives are all too valuable to the cause we are engaged in, to throw them away lightly."

The sudden report of a pistol in the adjoining room startled them, and for a few moments they could not conceive what it was for. The conversation of the soldiers, however, soon informed them.

"Is it alight?" said one.

"Yes, all's right, I put in a large loose wadding, and that always comes out in a blaze. There it is."

"Oh, that's glorious—there goes the powder. We shall be different beings now. How the flame roars up the chimney; I'll warrant now there has not been such a cheerful blaze here for a long time."

"Not for a year," said another. "I've seen the house shut up for a length of time, and often wondered whose it was."

"Shall we find any cavaliers in it?"

"Not one. There's some mistake in the whole affair, I take it."

How the flame roared and crackled up the chimney, now bringing down by its pressure huge flakes of old soot.

CHAPTER XI.

MORE PERIL.—THE DESPERATE RESOLUTION.

AFTER the fire was fairly lighted, there was among the cavaliers a death-like stillness. They were all too deeply interested in watching what species of effect it was likely to have upon the little room in which they were, to make any remarks to each other, even in the low and guarded whispers in which they had been conversing. The troopers, however, who had so unconsciously spread so much alarm among the cavaliers, were more noisy than ever. The cheerful bright crackling blaze of the fire, seemed to have quite an exhilirating effect upon their spirits.

"A capital notion of yours this was, Stevenson," said one.

"Yes," added another, "he deserves the most of the fire, for the idea of kindling one at all."

"In that case then," said another, "the only way I can think of to give him his deserts, is to set him on it."

A roar of laughter followed this little bit of troopers' wit, and certainly Cromwell's dragoons only wanted the arrival of the refreshments from Bird-cage-walk to make their satisfaction tolerably complete. But the fire had not been lit many minutes before it began sufficiently to show how serious an affair it could and would be to the cavaliers. Thick wreaths of the most dense and strong-smelling vapour from the damp wood that was piled upon the grate, made their way into the little apartment, and although these wreaths of smoke ascended, yet they tainted the air as they did so. Moreover, if they had continued they would soon have had the effect of vitiating the entire atmosphere of the place. Another evil, too, began to show itself. The cavaliers became each moment conscious of a highly increasing temperature, and they were justly enough afraid of its momentary increase, while there was no possible means of ventilation in the place. They had all been rather cold, and at first this increase of temperature was very far indeed from being disagreeable, but its steady increase soon made it dreaded. The smoke, too, began to effect the lungs of some of them, and to bring on a troublesome cough, which it was one of the most difficult of things in the world to repress at

[THE CAVALIERS STRATAGEM.—THE DRUGGED WINE.]

the same time that it was one of the most dangerous to indulge in. It was wlls that the boisterous mirth of the soldiers was of a character to drown other souned of a less noticcable character.

"More wood!" cried a trooper, "more wood! we must never let a wood fire go down, or it will pop out when you are least aware of it."

The heavy blows of a sword slashing down some woodwork in the room quickly followed the demand, proving that if more wood was wanted, those who called for it were by no means very particular where it came from. The grate was piled u again, and the flames being by such means partially smothered, volleys of smoke found their way into the room where the cavaliers were each moment getting into a worse position. It really became now a serious object of consideration; whether they should remain any longer as they were, or make a bold attempt to free themselves by a rush into the room where the troopers were. The grate, as we have said, revolved upon a centre, but a vigorous push from the cavaliers' side would easily throw it completely over, and leave an opening through which one man at a time could make his way sword in hand. The only probability of accomplishing such a manœuvre with safety lay in the likelihood of the upset of the grate sufficiently surprising the soldiers to give time for several cavaliers to reach the room where they were. Sir Walter Cardwell held a whispered conference with his companions round the table. They had scarcely begun the council, however, when a loud knocking came upon the street-door of the house in which the soldiers were.

"Is that hope for us?" said Lord Sefton.

"No," said Sir Walter Cardwell, "I'm afraid we have no friends in London who know of our peril; and I am tolerably certain that if they did know of it, we have no friends who would come in such a way."

"What can it be?"

"Hush!"

A loud laugh from the soldiers rang through the house, and they heard one cry out loudly,—

"Here they come with a well-filled basket."

"It is the party from the barracks," said Sir Walter. "We must do nothing while they stay, for in such small numbers, three or four men make a powerful and rather alarming reinforcement."

"True—true," said one, "yet we are losing strength here."

"Hush! Let us hear what they have to say. Perchance they bring some orders that may prove of importance to us in our deliberation."

The party with the provisions made its way to the room, and one said,—

"Well comrades, have you anything to report?"

"Nothing but that we are hungry."

"We have brought what will soon mend that. Where's your officer?"

"Asleep, wrapped up in his cloak, in the next room, and to our thinking, he is not so well off as we are, for he has no fire, while we are enjoying ourselves amazingly, as you see."

"Upon my word you are comfortable indeed."

"We are—we are. What have you brought us?"

"Bread and cheese."

"Cheese?"

"Aye, truly, and the Colonel says he hopes you will say an appropriate grace before partaking of it."

"Grace?"

"Yes, you know him!"

"Confound him. Bread and cheese! Well, well, it can't be helped. What has he sent us to drink?"

"Nothing."

"Nothing?"

"No. He says he has no doubt you will find a water-butt in the lower part of the house, and as there has been heavy rains lately, he dare say it is full."

The cavaliers could not see, but they could imagine from the silence that ensued, the looks of blank dismay that sat upon the faces of the troopers at this, to them, piece of most dismal intelligence regarding the drink they had fully expected. Sir Walter Cardwell could hardly forbear a smile, as he whispered,—

"What a pity we cannot supply them with something stronger than they expected from the barracks."

"That is a good idea," said Lord Wilton. "If I can but make Waller hear me quietly, I don't see but what it may be made something of."

"Indeed ?"

"How ?—how ?"

"Why, what is to hinder Waller from finding somebody who will supply them with drink that may be medicated so as to steep their senses in forgetfulness. We don't want to take their lives. They are but the poor instruments of a higher power. All we want is to escape their clutches."

"True. True."

"Be still, then, while I ascertain if Waller is within hearing ; I told him to destroy the tube, lest his house should be searched, and he may have done so."

"Not probable," said Sir Walter Cardwell ; "I never knew Waller do anything very hasty yet, and he will not begin now."

"Waller—Waller," whispered Lord Wilton, through the tube.

"Here," was the reply. "How are you all ?"

"Half dead. The tube is open."

"Yes, but a hot blast of air comes through, as if from a furnace."

"In that air we live, Waller. But the troopers in the next room to us want drink ; can you manage to gratify them with something stronger than common ?"

"Surely."

"Can you find anybody to do it ?"

"Yes."

"Then you will save us, Waller ?"

"I see my way now. It shall be done. Hold out for a little time if you can possibly, and all will be well. Do you know Harrison, the player ?"

"Oh surely."

"Well, he is lodging in my house. If you only tell me that he may be trusted, I will open the matter to him, and he will be of the most material assistance."

"What is your opinion of him ?"

"An honest fellow, who hates the Puritans as the devil is said to hate the New Testament."

"Trust him by all means."

"Good. I will waste no time. Listen to what takes place, and choose your own opportunity of emerging from where you are. There are some half dozen troopers, with loaded carbines, parading the street, so make the best of your situation. The back of the house is well guarded likewise."

"Where is Adams ?"

"Slinking about. At times he holds by the railings of the houses and looks in at the dusky windows. Then he walks down the street as if going away, but he soon returns again, and, take him for all in all, I never in all my life saw such an absolute picture of an unhappy restless wretch."

"It is well to be cautious, Waller."

"It is indeed."

Waller left the end of the tube, and Lord Wilton came back to his companions to report to them what had happened. The prospect of something being done for their release from the painful situation in which they were, inspired them all with fresh courage ; and by the advice of one of their number, who was more of a natural philosopher than the rest, they all sat down upon the floor, when they were certainly enabled to breathe a much purer nature of air than above. They were all now in the greatest possible anxiety to listen to any indications of Charles having commenced some movement for their deliverance. The soldiers in the mean time continued their riotous conversation. The bread and cheese were partaken of amid much grumbling, and an expedition was sent down stairs in search of water, but returned empty-handed, with information that the spout which had conducted rain-water into a cistern was broken down, and there was not a drop consequently to be had. A discussion ensued as to whether or not leave was to be asked of the officer to go to some neighbouring tavern and order drink, but as the officer was asleep, the more prudent portion of them, and we may suppose the least thirsty, negatived the notion as being dangerous.

"And so," said one, "we are to be parched up with thirst, for Heaven knows how long, in this abominable place!"

"I am nearly dead," said another.

"And I," cried a third; "ever since lighting the fire I have had a mouth full of wood ashes, and am half choked for want of something to wash them down. What the deuce shall we do?"

Bang! came a knock at the street-door. The soldiers were all silent for a few moments, and the sergeant assuming the command, said,—

"A couple of you go and see who it is. You, 23 and 24, take your carbines."

The two troopers at once marched from the room, and before they reached the door another heavy bang announced the impatience as well as the temerity of the visitor. What happened below the cavaliers had no means of knowing, but in the course of a few minutes they heard a sort of shuffling noise upon the stairs beyond the room, and then the door being flung open the two soldiers dragged in somebody who was remonstrating against such violence.

"Gentlemen! Gentlemen! what will my master say? Good gentlemen, don't, say what you like, and do what you like, so that you leave alone the bottled ale. I can assure you, gentlemen, I am taking it to a sick person, and I thought this was the house. I knocked by mistake, gentlemen."

"Nonsense!" said one of the soldiers who had been to the door, and was hardly able to speak for laughter. "It's no mistake."

"What is it all about?" said the sergeant.

"Why simply this. When we got to the door, this fellow said, 'I have brought the ale;' upon which we handed him up stairs, with this basket of his."

"Yes, but gentlemen, you forget I said I brought the ale for Mrs. Lightbody. Ah! you know I said that."

"Well, that's me?" said the sergeant.

"You, sir? Body o' me, you don't say so?"

"Ay, to be sure. Come, give out the ale. You have a goodly lot of it?"

"Only a dozen bottles, gentlemen, with which I pray you let me go. It is strong ale, sparkling, singing, luxurious ale, and smells like a nosegay. Don't drink it, gentlemen. It will get into your heads."

"Ha, ha, ha!" roared the soldiers.

The basket was seized hold of, and the dozen bottles soon placed upon the temporary table in a goodly row. The porter began to say,—

"Oh, dear. Oh, dear! I shall be discharged. Oh, oh, oh! I tell you its strong ale, and will get into your heads, as sure as a gun. It's only Mrs. Lightbody, who can at all stand it."

"Don't be a fool," said the sergeant. "We will drink it."

"But Mrs. Lightbody is ill."

"Then we will drink her health."

"But she is a great person."

"So is Corporal Simes there. He is six feet three in his boots. Gentlemen, we will consider this as a dispensation of Providence if you please. There's a bottle each for us, so fire away."

The sergeant, with a blow of his sword, struck off the neck of one of the bottles, and with more or less success, according to their dexterity or clumsiness, the others followed his example, amid much roaring and laughing, for never were men more delighted than were those troopers, at this most unexpected supply in the shape of drink that had come to them."

"Beau—tiful!" said the sergeant.

"Capital!" cried the men.

"I am lost!" said the porter. "I'm a ruined individual! Oh, what will become of me? What can I do?"

"Nothing, but tell your master how pleased Mrs. What's-her-name was with the ale, and that she wants another dozen."

"You don't say so?"

"Why now," said the serjeant, putting on an air of great sageness, "this fellow is, after all, little better than an idiot. If he had his wits properly about him, he would be able to invent a hundred excuses to account for the loss of the ale. It is princely liquour—fit for a general, comrades, I—I never—(hiccup) tasted anything like it."

" Nor—I—"

" Hurrah!—Give us a toast, you mean booby—put another bit of wood on—on—. Eh? What do you say?"

The serjeant had emptied his bottle, and he fell forward, very narrowly missing the fire in his progress. Two of the men were likewise overpowered, and the one got a little suspicious, and cried,—

" Help! help! my head swims.—There's—something in—in—in the ale——"

Down he fell to the floor. Another made a weak attempt to reach his carbine, but sunk helpless in the attempt so to do. Three minutes elapsed, and the sham ale-porter was standing in the room in an attitude of listening, while around him lay the insensible forms of the whole twelve soldiers:

" The narcotic has done it's duty," he said. " If the officer don't awake now, for a few minutes, all will be well enough, and Master Waller's friends will be able to make some effort at an escape shortly."

CHAPTER XII.

MR. DASHALL'S FAMILY IN AN UPROAR.

THE events which we have related as occurring during the progress of that most eventful night when the cavalier took refuge in the house of the draper, were such as by no means tended to mollify the feelings of Mr. Dashall's family. It will be remembered that the cavalier, after in the most faintly excusable manner making his way into the bed-room of Jemima, the niece of the aforesaid Dashall, did there and then overhear her mention the name of Alfred, and then, having perpetrated the social offence of stealing a kiss without leave, he intimated that it was Alfred who was the midnight intruder. Whether or not the cavalier, who called himself Jocelyn, had any further idea or intention in such a matter than mere sport, we cannot just now say. It is, however, just possible that he thought by passing himself off for Alfred—the Alfred of Jemima's dream—he might induce her not to make the alarm continuous, which in her first apprehension she had commenced with so peculiarly vivid a scream. At all events, he had done mischief, for in that delerious state between sleeping and waking which tne young maiden was in she really believed that there had been an invasion of the sanctity of her chamber by him to whom she had given her young heart, and who ought to have been as mindful of her honour as he was of her affections. If the reader be one of the fairer and gentler sex, she can well imagine with what a pang of regret poor Jemima came slowly to the conclusion that her idol, Alfred, was not the perfect and honourable character she had curtained in her heart of hearts. No wonder, then, that Jemima got up in the morning tearful, and with evident signs of distress. Mrs. Dashall got up vexed and furious, for, after the departure of Joceylin, the two men who had made such exertions to get into the house, and then, after all, let their prey escape them in so simple a manner, had run up the stairs at headlong speed. When they reached the landing from which opened Mr. Dashall's bed-room, they made no more ado, but dashed open the door, and rushed in one over the other. In vain Mrs. Dashall screamed and cried murder! In vain Dashall shut himself up in a cupboard, and nearly fainted away. The two men rushed under the bed with a precipitation that was truly awful. What on earth they could want there, was the greatest mystery to Mrs. Dashall. She could not helf feeling that so indecorous a proceeding was truly dreadful, and no wonder that she jumped out of bed, and dealt one of them, as he emerged, a blow with the dressing-glass, which demolished it, and left the frame like a collar round the man's neck. A large washhand basin was the next weapon laid hold of by the infuriated lady, and that proved itself the weaker vessel against the head of the other man, for it smashed in pieces with the concussion. For a few moments then, so sudden had been this attack, that Mrs. Dashall really had her two foes quite at her mercy, and she took care, by the aid of rather a heavy pair of fire tongs, to make the most of the opportunity, and to "improve the occasion," as the saints say. Flesh and blood might stand all this for a short time, but bones could not, and the men began rather vigorously to act upon the defensive. Mrs. Dashall beat a retreat to the bed, and shrieked for aid. A light flashed upon the scene, and a servant made her appearance from the lower part of the house with a candle in her hand, and a look of blank surprise upon her stupid, stolid looking face.

"Lor! what's the matter?"

There was a sudden cessation of hostilities, and the two men looked at each other, and at the servant, and then at Mrs. Dashall. At last they looked at all they could see of that lady, which, as faithful historians, we are bound to declare was her feet—for she had gathered the clothing of the bed in such profusion about her head and face, that she left the lower part of the bed bare.

"Murder!—fire!—murder!—thieves!—fire!—fire!"

"Fetch the hangines," said the servant.

"Why what the deuce," said the man upon whose head a great bump had been made with the washhand-basin, "what the deuce is the meaning of all this? I'm half murdered."

"And so am I," said the other. "Curse you all. I'm full of bits of broken looking-glass, that some fiend has cracked over my head."

"Well, rally," said the servant, "if I didn't think I heard somethink. As I'm a sinner, says I, somethinks a going on, so I gets up, and up I comes to see whatever it could be."

"Oh, Sue—Sue!" cried Mrs. Dashall, "is that you?"

"Yes, um."

"What do you see?"

"Your two legs, um."

"Gracious!"

"Have mercy upon us all, Amen!" said Mr. Dashall, popping his head out of the cupboard, for he thought that murder was going on.

"Why who are you?" cried one of the men.

"Simon Dashall, draper and hosier."

"Then we are done!"

"I'm glad of that," said Sue, "you can go now. I don't know what made you begin, but, howsomedever, rally, as you is done, why go your ways away at once."

"There's been a man in your house," said one of the intruders to Dashall.

"I know it," said Dashall.

"What's become of him?"

"How should I know."

"Then what do you know about it?"

"Just this much, gentlemen, that all night long people have been running under the bed, in at one side and out at the other, and up and down stairs like so many lamplighters. That's all I know about it, and all I can say is, that I'm now so bewildered, that I don't know whether I'm on my head or on my heels, or whether I'm wide awake or it's all a dream."

"At all events, we have missed our man," said one of the officers, for such indeed they really were.

"And pray who was your man, gentlemen?" said Dashall.

"Humph!" said one of the men.

"Ha!" said the other.

"Lor!" said Sue, "there was two of 'em, rally."

"Hark ye, Mr. Dashall," said one, "if such another party should come to your house, we don't mind buying £50 worth of drapery if you hold him tight till we come. If you had laid hands upon the man we seek, it would have been the best night's work ever you did in all your life."

"But who was he?" cried Mrs. Dashall, whose curiosity had got the better of every other feeling. "Who was it? Tell me directly."

"Missus has drawed in her legs," said Sue.

"Oh, you vile hussey. Who was the man, I say? Tell me directly who it was."

"Oh, certainly, mum," said one of the men, "is there anything else you'd like to know? Come along, Finch, come along."

"Ah," said Finch, gloomily, "it's no use staying [here] now, Joliffe. Not a bit. My usual luck. A cracked crown and nothing for it. Come along—come along."

"You won't tell me who it was?" cried Mrs. Dashall.

"Here she comes," said Finch. Confound that woman!"

The disappointed officers ran down stairs as hard as they could, for they really fancied that Mrs. Dashall was upon the point of springing out of bed to make another attack upon them.

"Rally," said Sue, "as I said to myself says I, I goes and sees what's amiss up stairs, says I, and I goes."

The two men left the house, slamming the street-door to behind them with a vengeance that shook the whole premises. It is not to be wondered at, that after this the temper of Mrs. Dashall should have undergone rather an acctous fermentation. The remainder of the night was spent in reproaching Dashall with his pusillanimity, and by giving him sundry pokes and punches in the back, to avoid which, he gradually got so close to the edge of the bed, that at length he fell out upon the floor. Upon this, Mrs. Dashall said he was always falling out of bed on purpose to annoy her, and he should not come in any more that night. Dashall did not make the faintest resistance. He had long ago given up all idea of doing that, and he retreated to a sofa in another room, with all the meekness of a lamb in special good humour.

"She's a fine woman," said Dashall to himself, "a very fine woman—a woman of amazing abilities. What a pity it is that her temper is just so—so—just a little, in a manner of speaking."

Thus passed the remainder of that most eventful night at the Dashall's—a night of which none in the house knew the full importance yet—nor did he, Jocelyn, the young cavalier, think that its events would yet come before him in a shape anything but pleasant. They did do so, but we must not anticipate. At breakfast, Mrs. Dashall was dignified and gloomy. She did not do anything very particular according to Dashall, for beyond throwing a red herring in his face and a cup of tea after it, she was peaceable enough. A little spirit of exaggeration had taken possession of her regarding the night's proceedings. Instead of stating to Mrs. Whistler, the butcher's wife, during the morning, that two men had bounced under the bed, she stated that six men had bounced into it. That was all. But it was Jemima who really suffered from the night's proceedings, and if ever real heartfelt sorrow was upon a fair and ingenuous countenance, it was upon that of the draper's beautiful niece on the morning after; she fully believed that Alfred had made so bad a use of a privilege he had of coming to the house without the cognizance of the draper himself. By climbing some rails, and letting himself in at a kitchen-door which was not often used, Alfred certainly had had some private interviews with Jemima, in the lower part of the draper's house. His honour had been trusted, not to take, or attempt to take, the smallest advantage of such a concession, nor had he; but now, to all appearance, he was most guilty. Perhaps, had a full and fair explanation of all the events of the previous night, so far as they were known, taken place at the draper's breakfast-table in the morning, Jemima might have found cause to suspend her judgment, but no such fair explanation or conversation took place, and Jemima was left to her own dismal thoughts, and painful surmises of her lover's perfidy. It is, however, and has always been, and will, we suppose, always be until the end of the world, a melancholy fact, that

"The course of true love runs not smooth ;"

although now, in these days of gliding airy locomotion, it is a world of pities that Cupid is still as great a laggard in improvement as a Whig minister. We can only hope that the fair and the virtuous will, in the end, be the happy; although it is still to be mourned that, from the first, any crosses should beset the love of a fair heart, or any thorns and briars stand in the way of those who invoke love's pilgrimage ; but we must suppose it to be part and parcel of the primeval curse, that no pleasure—no joy is to be sought, but through pain, if it be a pure pleasure and a pure joy ; for we find, if we give the subject a moment's consideration, that pain is always the subsequent of impure joys and pleasures. But we must leave these loving and saddened birds now for a while, to mingle with much more stormy scenes, and again request the reader's kind companionship to that house in Westminster, where so deeply interesting a scene was being enacted—a scene which was in its results calculated to raise upon the brow of Cromwell one of the angriest flushes that ever rested there.

CHAPTER XIII.

THE TEMPLE GARDEN.

Those who are familiar with London and its localities, know something of the Temple, that ancient town, for a town it almost is of itself, which, despite the various changes that the great metropolis has undergone, has still preserved all the essentials of its old state. The houses still show their dingy fronts—the attics still have their old gable ends, and in many cases picturesque roofs, while the interiors of many of those houses are decorated by the art of the carver, in a manner that would play havoc with modern specimens. Some of the old ceilings are perfect treasures of art. But it is not with the houses in the old Temple that we have to do, nor with the race of thieves in the shape of lawyers, who have displaced the race of thieves in the shape of priests militant, that we now have to do. We would only invite attention to the garden by the banks of the Thames, appertaining to the Temple, upon the trim walks of which have paced so many of England's notables. This garden was then the haunt of lovers. Alas! how has it fallen! Where now would be heard within its dingy precincts the soft accents of affection? When would those who loved wisely or unwisely, ever think of proceeding to such a spot to breathe their vows? If they did, they might expect to be peered at by some old hag affecting to read, but really plotting mischief in conjunction with another evil spirit. No—fond and true hearts, there is not sufficient purity in the Temple Garden atmosphere now, to render it a fitting place for your vows. But, at the time of which we write, things were somewhat different, and gentle maidens would at times meet bashful youths in that green spot. It was green then, and not that dingy libel upon vegetation which it now appears. We have said thus much to account for the actions of Jemima, the niece of Mr. Dashall; for if we had not ventured into something like an explanation as we have, the actions of that young lady would appear to be rather of the incomprehensible order. Behold, then, this fair, and gentle, and loving creature in her own room ; that room, which had been but so lately profaned by the presence of one who thought it manly and gallant to insult a weakness it would have been noble to protect. We will look at her sweet face—aye, and at her fair eyes too, despite the blinding tears that strive to hide them. She is making up a packet, and as she makes it up she gives a half-frenzied utterance to the thoughts that, like demons, are busy at her heart—

"Yes," she said, " he shall have all back, and I will ask him but one favour,

THE LOVERS' MISUNDERSTANDING.

and that will be, to forget me—never again to utter my name. That will be all I
shall now ask of Alfred. Oh ! why did he ever say that he loved me ?"

A torrent of tears checked her utterance, and she was compelled to pause in
what she was about, until she had somewhat recovered from her emotion. People
talk of the desolation of hearts by death—of desert places in the wild wastes of
untrodden continents, but what desolation—what desert can come near that of the
heart of a young trusting gentle girl, who has loved and erected an idol, to
worship in her veriest heart, only some day to find that it is something less than

human ? Such was Jemima's condition. In about five minutes she recovered, however, sufficiently to proceed with what she had been about. Oh, mournful task ! It was to make a small parcel of any little *gage d' amour* which from time to time Alfred had presented to her—she was that morning resolved to give all back to him at the moment that she asked of him the favour of forgetfulness. It is needless to describe these little articles. They were trifles in themselves, but around each Love had wreathed his own bewitching atmosphere, and unnumbered blessings twined themselves in heavenly sweetness about them. Alas ! what were they now ? Heart-rending remembrances of that which was, but is not—a love pure and beautiful. She felt that henceforth there was a chasm between her and Alfred.

> "————They stood apart,
> Like rocks which had been rent asunder.
> A dreary sea now flows between,
> But neither heat, nor frost, nor thunder
> Shall wholly do away I ween
> The marks of that which once hath been !"

And so it was with her, for she leant her head upon her hands, and her long fair tresses hung like a glossy veil around her, as she said—
"I shall love no more ! The spring of my affections is gone—I shall love no more. My heart's young joy has known no summer sunshine, but from early blossom has dropped into

> "The sere and yellow leaf."

I am desolate, most desolate."

The neighbouring church clock pealed forth the hour of twelve, and she started.—From that hour until one, she had been accustomed to know that she should always find Alfred in the Temple Gardens. Would he be there that day ? It was a question ; but she was resolved to go upon her last pilgrimage to that spot which had become endeared to her by a thousand gentle recollections. — Oh, those blessed memories were now turned to gall and bitterness, but she felt that now she owed a sacred duty to herself, and she did hope that Heaven would in pity give her strength to perform it. If Heaven did not in mercy give her that strength, and she should fail through weakness in vindicating her honour well, and in casting what was unworthy from her heart, she at least would feel that she had made a great and praiseworthy attempt—that was something. She hurriedly completed the arrangements of her little packet. She took one last bewildering look at its contents, and then she hurriedly tied around it a silken thread, and hiding it under her cloak, she at once left the house by the private door to proceed to the Temple. Jemima took her way down Milford-lane, and so on through well-known courts and alleys into the seat of legal learning and chicanery. Oh, how her heart beat as she neared the garden gate. The guardians of this *oasis* in the Temple were not then so particular in their stern dominion over the gate as they are now-a-days. This is an exclusive age ; but Jemima had but to push the iron screen open, and to walk into the garden. How full of doubts and fears is love ! Before she had taken two steps within the garden she began to ask herself if the course she was now adopting was really the best, or if she had not better have stayed at home, and calmly refused ever again to see Alfred. What should she do ? Even as she asked herself the question, and debated with herself upon the propriety of returning, she had sped forward to the long walk like a startled fawn. Then she heard a hurried footstep behind her—a voice pronounced her name, and turning she beheld Alfred with both his hands extended, and upon his countenance a smile of such truthfulness, joy, and sincerity, that Jemima, believing him to be guilty of the outrage that had made such an impression upon her mind, was positively amazed that he could now look as he did.

"Ah, my Jemima, dear one," he said, "I began to fear you would not come.

Ah, how fertile love is in his torments! I fancied that by some little harmless gallantry I might have given offence to you."

Jemima shuddered. She knew, at least she had heard, that gallantry was the word which acted as a cover to vice in all its grossness; but that he, Alfred, should attempt to excuse himself in such a way—and certainly, what he unfortunately said sounded something like an excuse—for the intrusion into her chamber, transcended all she had expected.

"Alfred," she said, "can this be really you?"

"Really I!" he replied. "Oh, Jemima, why that look of sadness?"

"Alfred, you said you loved me, and you persuaded me that——"

Her feelings overcame her, she could say no more, but letting fall at his feet the little packet she had made up, was about to turn from the spot, when she recollected that it was necessary, at all events, to tell him of what it consisted. For this purpose she did manage, when a few few paces from the bewildered youth, to turn, and say—

"Take back all that you gave, and forget me."

"Take back—forget you, Jemima? No—no——"

"Yes, Alfred. Farewell!"

"Gracious Heaven! what is this? Jemima, will you kill me? What have I done? What fault have I committed, that you should treat me thus? Oh, no—no, you are joking with me. You are playing with a passion, which is so much a part my life, that to play with it, is to sport with my existence. In mercy, Jemima, let me see you smile."

"I do not think, Alfred, I shall smile again for a long—long time. They do say, that time heals all wounds, and it is possible that I may forget you, as I ask you from henceforward to forget me."

"Forget you? Oh, those horrible words, no—no. Only tell me, Jemima, one thing. Do you love another? If so, leave me at once, and you will never see me more. It is all I ask of you, if this dreadful scene be serious. Do you love another?"

"No."

"Then I am saved."

"Saved?"

"Yes; I will not—cannot—dare not forget you, for by so doing I should forget myself. No, Jemima. There is some mystery in all this, which I cannot solve, but it will be the duty of my life to discover it. Only tell me what I have done, or what I am supposed to have done."

"You have been—gallant!"

Poor Alfred looked bewildered, as well indeed he might. The conduct of Jemima was, to him, one of the most incomprehensible things in all the world. Merely to charge him with being gallant, was to him, one of the oddest incidents he had ever encountered, but when he looked in the pale, subdued face of the suffering girl, he could not for one moment doubt but that she was perfectly sincere in what he said, and that one of those misadventures which so effectually prevent

"The even course of fond hearts' passion"

had fallen in his way. But what on earth could it be? In most such cases there was a something that might lead to a conjecture, but here there was nothing. All was bewilderment and chaos, and when he tried to unravel it, he could but change the words, and call it chaos and bewilderment. He looked like a man in a dream.

"Concience stricken!" thought Jemima.

"She is mad!" thought Alfred.

They stood gazing at each other for the space of about three minutes in utter silence. Oh, what a three minutes of agony that was to both of them. At length, turning with tottering steps, Jemima essayed to leave the place, uttering, as she did so, the one word—

"Farewell"

This roused Alfred from his trance. He sprung before her, and interrupted her passage, as with a desperate earnestness he thus spoke to her—

"Jemima! You know I love you. At least, you have had good reason to believe in the sincerity of my attachment to you, and now you suddenly meet me with a chilling coldness, and tell me that I ought to forget you. Listen to me. By loving you as I have loved you, I gave you some rights—but at the same time, I required some myself."

"I do not understand you."

"But you shall. One of those rights I so required, was the right of demanding that you should be sincere and candid with me. Answer me, Jemima. Are you so?"

"I am sufficiently. Farewell for ever!"

"Jemima!"

"Sir."

"One moment."

"Will you stop me by force from leaving this place when I please?"

"No—no—I——"

He fell back a pace or two, and Jemima gliding past him in a moment, left the Temple Garden, and was some distance on her route to her uncle's house before Alfred recovered his equanimity sufficiently to make up his mind what to do. He then picked up from the ground, where it had hitherto lain, the little packet which Jemima had brought with her, and cast at his feet. He thrust it unopened into the breast of his apparel.

"Be it so," he said. "That dream is over. If I love again, may I be so played with, and so duped. Farewell then, since such is your verdict, Jemima. Farewell for ever! I will obey your last injunction by forgetting you."

Any one who at that moment had seen the young man, and noted the despairing action of his hands, might have well guessed, though they heard not what he said, that at the time he was setting himself a task far beyond his powers to accomplish. With a disordered mien and a tottering step he left the Temple Garden. There was now no garden for him in this world.—Rank weeds, and the blasts of desolation, had for ever, as he thought, choked up and made a wilderness of the garden of his heart! Jemima was false. What more could the world offer to him in the shape of desolation or despair, now that she, upon whose faith he would have placed his salvation, was to him no more?

CHAPTER XIV.

THE MURDER ON THE BRIDGE.

Upon that night, a circumstance happened upon Old London Bridge, or rather in one of the rotten old tumble-down houses that stood upon it, which it is necessary to the progress of our story we should relate, inasmuch as it will, by being now recorded, not interrupt the even course of other matters, which still could not be entirely explained without a knowledge of this incident. One of these houses, the lower part of which was a miserable shop, where old arms and armour were ostensibly the traffic, was inhabited by a man named Allsops. Old Allsops, as he was called, was rather a singular character, and many strange rumours were rife concerning him and his pursuit. There were some who asserted that there was no species of unlawful work that this old man was not ready to engage in, while others again, who were not wonder-mongers to so great an extent, simply designated him as an usurer, although in reality, if he were truly one of that tribe, he could not be much worse. At all events, Old Allsops ostensibly dealt in arms and armour, and there, from morn until night, and from night until morn again, was he to be found in his dismal house upon the bridge, which he in reality never left. There were two modes of entrance and exit to his house. One of these was from the causeway of the bridge, and the other by a step staircase up one of the piers of the bridge; and it was by this latter route that many of Allsops' customers seemed most to delight to come to his weather-beaten ricketty house. The clock of St. Paul's had struck twelve, and Old Allsops, after listening for a little time to the loud wind which that night was dashing the river craft one against the other, carefully fastened up his house, and dragging a miserable old mattress out of a cupboard, bethought him of retiring to rest for the night.

"No visitors to-night," he mumbled, "no visitors to-night. If the lads had intended transacting any business, they would have let me know of it long before now. All's right. No business to-night. Well, well, the more to-morrow, perhaps."

Thus then, having given up all hopes of any visitors, Old Allsops, who was in reality waiting for the river pirates who brought at times booty to him to be disposed of, arranged his mattress and fairly lay down to rest. One struck by St. Paul's, and the old man heard a whistle, coming as if from the water at the foot of the step stairs leading from his house to the stream. He half raised himself to listen. The whistle was repeated, and he sprung to his feet.

"It is one of them," he said. "I must go. If they once had any doubts of finding me here, they might go now and then to some one else. Oh, I must go—I must go."

Round his neck, even while he slept, he had appended to a string a small ivory whistle, and opening a little window next the river, he projected his head and the whistle out, and blew a shrill blast.

"Hilloa!" said a voice, "Allsops?"

"Yes, yes. One of the lads. What, ho?"

"Nine!" said the voice.

"Oh, nine. Then it is you, Jem Salmon. By our Lady, I did not know you by your voice. I am coming. I am coming.—Be patient, my child, and I come.—Yes—yes, I come.—No impatience, my child; no impatience."

The old man with trembling hands got a light, which he placed upon the window-sill, and then he found a tall narrow door in the wall, and uncoiling a rope, he cast the end of it down the outer stairs, so that it might serve as a guide to the person who had come to make the somewhat perilous ascent.

"Up—up," said Allsops, "up and be quick. They say that the new Lord Mayor is a sharp man, and a cunning. But he don't find us out, my child.—No —no—no."

The old scoundrel, for a scoundrel he was in more ways than one, chuckled to himself as he uttered these words, and began to make up a fire of dry wood upon the hearth, adding as he did so—

"They always pay cheerfully enough for the fire and the light.—Ha! ha!—and for much else beside. Ha! ha!—so they do."

While Allsops was thus engaged, the person who had represented himself as No. 9, was slowly ascending, from a small wherry closely moored to the pier of the bridge, the narrow steep staircase leading to the old man's house. In about half a minute the visitor passed through the tall narrow door into the chamber, but he closed it again so suddenly and abruptly behind him that it not only made a loud noise, but puffed out the light Allsops had illuminated.

"Hilloa! hilloa!" said the old man, "what do you mean by that?"

No answer was returned to him, and the sticks he had been coaxing into a flame upon the hearth, had not yet sufficiently done their duty to give him light enough to see a single object in the room, although with eyes sharpened by suspicion he glared around him.

"Where are you?" he cried, "where are you?"

All was still as the grave. Old Allsops was getting a little alarmed, and with trembling hands he relighted the lamp. It cast a fitful glare around it, and

Allsops saw that the room contained no one but himself.—His knees smote each other with terror, and his few scanty locks almost bristled upon his head.—The old man had no religion, but he had abundance of superstition.

" What's this?" he groaned, " what's this?—I'm sure; yes, I'm quite sure, I heard some one come and—and—some one slammed the door.—What—what is it?"

There was a door close to the side of the fire-place, which led into an inner room, and upon this Allsops now cast his eyes with a horrible misgiving that whoever it was, or whatever it was that visited him at that hour, might have glided past him in the dark, and gone into that room where he kept what he valued most on earth—his gold! The horror of such a thing as this happening, in a moment overcame all other feelings, and with a yell of despair the old man rushed to the door of the inner room, and violently opening it he stood upon the threshold. A few paces in front of him was a man attired in a horseman's cloak, with a large slouched hat and plume.

" Dominick," he said, " Dominick Allsops."

Every particle of colour fled from the old man's cheeks, and his mouth opened as if by some horrible convulsion. He just managed to utter the name—

" Gerald."

" Yes," said the stranger. Where is Anne?"

" Anne?" gasped Allsops, " Anne?"

" Yes, I ask you for an account of your trust. Where is Anne?"

" Where is Anne?" gasped Allsops. " He ain't dead!—and he asks me, where is Anne?"

The stranger fixed a basilisk-like glance upon old Allsops, and said—

" Do you know me?"

" I—I—do know you, I think. He comes here, and he asks where is Anne? and he ain't dead at all!—No—no—no."

" Where is Anne?"

The old man sunk upon his knees, with the light in his hand, and all he could say now was, in a melancholy voice—

" Spare me! spare me!"

" Yes, as you spared her."

" Oh, God! oh, God! I do not know where she is. Oh, do not ask me. I know nothing. I cannot tell you where she is."

" But you can tell me where she is not, and where she ought to be. It is here!"

The old man sobbed.

" I must tell you, then," said the stranger, " what it seems you forgot. You are my uncle, Allsops. Well, I know little of you, but I thought you human, at all events, and three years ago, at half an hour after midnight, I came to you here."

" Yes—yes—yes."

" I brought with me a young girl, aged fifteen. Old as you were, and seared as your heart was by worldly things, and by the love of gain, even you were struck by the magic of her wondrous beauty. You looked abashed before her. I told you that she was alone in the wide world, with none to love her but myself. I gave you gold, and told you to take care of her for me until I came to you again."

" Yes—yes—yes."

" Well, I am come. Where is Anne?"

" Oh, gracious! he comes, and ain't dead after all, and asks me where is Anne."

" Answer me, uncle. Do not repeat my words, but answer me the direct and plain question that I put to you."

" Have you heard nothing?"

" Nothing."

The old man breathed more freely, and then he said—

" She died.—Yes, she died, bless her young soul; she died, and I was at great charge with her illness and her burial, nephew.—Why do you look at me so? Could I prevent her from dying?"

"No."

"Well then, nephew, why are you angry with me? All you have to do is to pay me for the great expenses I have been at. 'Tis true you left me gold, but consider, three years is a long time to keep any one. Do not look so fierce; I tell you she died a year—aye—more than a year ago."

"Miserable trickster! How could you keep her three years, if death called before me, and took her from you more than a year ago? Now listen, uncle, I have heard a different story.—It is said that a profligate noble of the court saw her and coveted her."

"No—no—no. Oh no, Sir Amesdale never saw her."

"I never mentioned Sir Amesdale, but I'm glad that you have, uncle, for now I know my man; but to continue that which I have heard. It is said that you sold my heart's treasure to that man for £300, believing me to be dead, from a false rumour to that effect which reached your ears. Is that true?—If it be true, this is your last hour."

"No. Help! help!—No—mercy!—mercy!—Have mercy upon me. It is all false. All, all false. Oh, no—no, you would not murder me?"

"No; but I will sentence you for your black crime, and then be the executioner of the sentence. Do you confess your guilt, uncle?"

"Oh, no, no! I sell a young girl for three hundred pounds! I have not got three hundred shillings. I never saw—I never dreamt of so much money. It is all false; I tell you she is dead, and I will take you to her grave. Dig up the ghastly remains, and look at her——"

"Her remains are ghastly. She is dead, but——"

"But—what?"

"She laid a murderess's hands upon herself, uncle! But I have seen her since, and she said that she would see me here at one o'clock. Has she come?"

The old man struggled to his feet. The horror of the possibility of such an apparition visiting him, froze up his faculties, and although he cried—"Help, help! Watch, watch!" his voice did not get beyond a whisper as he did so. It was horrible to see one so near the grave, in the natural course of nature, in so fearful a state, but then we shall lose part of our commiseration when we know that he was to the full as guilty as the young stranger pictured him, aye to the full, and beyond it far.

"Coming here?" he now gasped. "Coming here? No, no, no! That would be too horrible—much too horrible. I fear I am getting old, and that my mind at times goes astray with me. Oh, have mercy upon me."

"Old man, if you had committed any ordinary offence—if you had robbed—slain your foe in anger—nay, if you had torn from the fatherless their last support to satisfy your grasping avarice—if you had aimed at my life by any foul means, I would, in the depth of my scorn, leave you to your conscience; but why, old man, did you destroy one of God's fairest and most beautiful creations?"

"No—no—no! It was not I. They—they came, and took her in the night."

"She screamed?"

"Yes—yes, she did scream."

"And she asked you rather to kill her, than let her be torn away by ruffian violence, even from such a home as this?"

"Yes—she—she did."

"While you held open the door with one hand, and the light with the other?"

The stranger drew a long rapier, the blade of which glistened in the light, while the old man's eyes convulsively glared upon it. He stepped towards the hoary ruffian, whose right hand—for in his left he held the light—was in his breast. Suddenly he drew that right hand out—a pistol was in its grasp. To level it at his nephew's breast, and to draw the trigger, was the work of a moment.

"Thus I save myself!" he said; "your body will find a grave in the black mud of the Thames, my brave nephew.—Mercy! Oh, I am lost!"

The pistol flashed in the pan.

"Yes," said the stranger, "you are lost."

As he spoke, he did in the heat and anger of the moment perhaps what, even with all his deep and awful provocation, he might yet have hesitated to do—he rushed upon the old man with his sword, and ran him through the body. Allsops was standing with his back against the door, leading to the steep staircase of the Thames, and the sword went through him, and dashed into the frail panel. With such force did the nephew give the thrust, that the richly inlaid hilt of the rapier struck the old man's heart. The door, frail at the best of times, was dashed from its hinges, and uncle, nephew, sword, and light, all went headlong, along with the door, down the steep staircase into the Thames. The shriek that the old man uttered was heard and commented upon by many persons upon both banks of the Thames. Indeed it was quite loud enough to make itself heard far beyond those precincts. It was the shriek of Death! It was only by a hair's breadth that the falling bodies escaped striking against the wherry, which was moored immediately below the staircase leading to Allsops' house. If they had struck it, not only would the wherry have been dashed to pieces, but the young man likewise, who had visited his bad uncle, with so fearful a retribution for his wickedness. As it was, however, Allsops, with the sword still sheathed in his body, and pinned as it were, to the door, floated down the Thames—a fearful spectacle. The young man, after touching the muddy bottom of the stream, rose again quickly, and being an admirable swimmer, he soon cleared the water from his eyes, and saw that his boat was riding safely, fastened to an iron ring in the pier of the bridge. His uncle had already got too far off in his passage down the river for the nephew to notice him, and he accordingly, fancying that the old man had reached the bottom, scrambled at once into his wherry.

"I regret," he said, "that things have turned out in the manner they have. Truly I did not intend to kill the old man, but to upbraid him with his conduct, and terrify him into giving me all the information he could about Anne. Alas! alas!—my hasty temper, I see, will yet bring me into acts that I deeply regret."

He pushed off into the stream, and rowed towards Blackfriars.—After all, he only felt a kind of regret at the manner of his old uncle's death.—He did not accuse himself much for the act.

CHAPTER XV.

THE ASTROLOGER.

THE fair Jemima was doomed to a morning of adventure. She did not reach home quite so easily as she had anticipated. When she left her lover in the Temple Gardens, one may well suppose the state of her mind. It was a complete chaos of contending emotions.

"Alfred is unworthy," she said to herself, "and I shall never love again. Since there is no faith in him, there can be no faith in man. No—no, henceforth love and I are strangers."

Alas! how little did Jemima yet know of herself. She loved Alfred still, and she could no more help loving him than she could help drawing the breath of life.

She reached Milford Lane in safety, and was proceeding onward, when she observed coming towards her on the same side of the way a couple of "swaggering companions," or bloods of the town, as they were then called,—rakes who set all law, morality, and common decency at defiance—fellows whom nothing had any effect upon but a sharp sword, in more skilful hands than their own. Now, for a young girl alone to escape insult, and perhaps worse, at the hands of such a pair, was a proposition not to be for a moment entertained; and accordingly Jemima's first impulse was to retrace her stepts, lest that by so doing she ran the chance of encountering Alfred, who might think that she was coming back to him, and that, her pride told her, would be something worse than a passing insult from the swaggering companions. Irresolute what to do, she paused a moment, and heard one of the bloods cry—

"A prize! a prize! a petticoat!—aye, and a face that would tempt Oliver himself, although the old rascal is so taciturn that he would not look at a pretty girl while in company with those crop-eared knaves of officers of his, or in sight of his very godly troopers; but report says that he is as gallant as any of us cavaliers when he imagines himself to be alone. What, hoa!

These last words were spoken with a nasal twang, strongly imitative of the Puritans, and his companion laughed boisterously as they both hurried on towards Jemima, who began to be much terrified. To advance or retract seemed to

Jemima equally bad, and she shrunk against a door, which was surrounded by wieldy sculptured ornaments, with the hope that the two ruffians would pass her with merely a remark or so ; but that they seemed not disposed to do.

"A Hebe ! a perfect Hebe! one who will be sure to find grace in the eyes of our merry Charles when he is restored to his throne. Such a one will not escape the lynx-eye of the king's favourite, who will not fail to report so much beauty so his Highness."

"By Jove, yes !" said the other. "Where is her equal? Not at old Noll's country seat, I reckon, eh? Come, my beauty —a kiss !"

"Stop ; let me be served first," said the other. "Now, pretty one, look at me, and say if ever you saw a handsomer fellow in a long summer's day ?"

As he spoke he was about to fling his arms round Jemima's neck.

"As you would wish to be thought a gentleman," she said, "pass on, sir, and molest me not."

"Molest thee not? When I pass such beauty 'chaos has come again;' so now——"

Before he could proceed to any further violence, the door, close to which Jemima had sought refuge, suddenly opened, a hand, armed with a stout cudgel, was thrust out, and such a crack came upon the head of one of the swaggering companions, that he rolled into the roadway and lay insensible. At the same moment Jemima was forcibly dragged into the passage, and the door was immediately closed. The most profound darkness reigned in the passage, and Jemima, although thankful for her release from the "bloods," began to have a hundred unknown fears and dreads in her breast at the possibility of her having fallen into worse hands than those without.

"Help ! help !" she said. "Oh, let me go to my house !"

"You're safe," said a mild voice, "and in gentle hands. Pase awhile in security, until those who insulted you have left the street. Fear nothing."

There was something assuring and pleasant in the very voice of the person who uttered these words ; and Jemima, in some measure recovering from her fright, was able to venture a reply.

"Accept my thanks," she said ; "but as those who would have insulted me have gone, allow me to go my way in peace now. I give you many thanks."

"Nay," said the voice, "your foes are not yet gone; but I can lull your fears by another mode of exit. Will you trust me?"

Jemima thought that if he who spoke were not trustworthy, it would avail her nothing to let him see that she suspected him, since she was in his power; while she thought, that an apparently firm and generous reliance often begot sincerity and fair dealing.

"Yes," she said, " I will trust you."

"You are right," said the voice. "Follow me ; and again I say, fear nothing."

A hand touched her, and held the tips of her fingers gently, and she was led forward a considerable distance in the dark ; then she heard a door opened, and a dim lamp, in a room to which it was the entrance, shed a ray of light upon a tall figure, who advanced two steps, as if to meet her and her conductor.

"All dark ?" said he who held her by the hand.

"Yes," said the other.

In an instant the light was extinguished, and the darkness seemed more profound than before. Her conductor led her, as she guessed, into the room, and then a voice said faintly—

"She will do, think you ?"

"Aye, transcendantly," replied Jemima's conductor, and then inclining his voice towards her, he continued, "lady, you can do us a favour if you please in return for that which we have done you. It is nothing from which you need shrink in the least; and yet, trifling as it is, you shall give your free consent, or it shall be forgotten."

"Ingratitude," said Jemima, "is a social sin I would not lightly be accused of, and if what you ask of me be of the character you say, and I find it such upon explanation, I freely consent."

"You shall judge for yourself," lady. "All that is required of you, is, that you will stand for a few moments on a particular spot with your head and face uncovered; and move not, let you see or hear what you may."

"This is most mysterious. I know not what to say."

"You shall not be forced or even importuned. Say that you refuse, and he who now addresses you will only regret that he has not succeeded in inspiring you with confidence in his unspotted honour. That will be a deep regret, but that will be the sole result."

Jemima felt as though she was being in some way outdone in generosity, and she now promptly replied :—

"I consent. God forgive you and help me, if there be ought wrong or deceitful in all this."

"Be tranquil. You will not recall the memory of your compliance with regret."

"I hope not."

"This way, fair one, an it please you. This way."

The hand quickly led her forward for some distance, and then she heard another door open and shut, and she found herself still in the dark, but the air around her was full of aromatic perfumes of the most delicious character. It was warm, too, and the astonished girl could scarcely forbear an exclamation of surprise as she found herself in so totally different a climate to that of the passage and the other room. There was something very delightful in the feel of the atmosphere—she heard too, or fancied that she heard a faint murmuring sound of voices, but of that she could not feel herself quite sure. Indeed, her senses were altogether in such a state of excitement that she was scarcely in a condition to separate the real from the unreal of her situation. The hand that held her by a gentle touch of her fingers now paused, and the same voice said, but in a much lower tone—

"Lady, having reached the appointed spot, will it please you to divest yourself of your head-gear for a few brief moments?"

Jemima had promised to comply with what was demanded of her, and she at once took off the small hat and silken net that confined her hair—it fell in luxuriant mosses upon her neck and shoulders.

"I am ready," she said.

"Let me then," added the voice, "implore you neither to move nor to speak, let you see what you may. You personate something more than human, and the more *statesque* you can make yourself appear the better. Do you comprehend me?"

"I do."

"A thousand thanks. Some way will be found of rewarding this great kindness. You are placing one under an obligation who will not forget it."

She made no reply to this, but she stood alone with her hands clasped before her, and unconsciously assuming an attitude of great beauty. She strained both eyes and ears to discover something from which she might judge of her situation, but the profound darkness in which she was baffled her eye-sight, although the measured discourse that she heard, and had begun to fancy only that she had heard, came again upon her ears. There was suddenly now a rustling sound, as though some heavy piece of drapery had been withdrawn, and then Jemima heard much more plainly the voices. One spoke as with a bantering tone, saying,—

"If you do give me such a sample of your art as you say you can give me, I will believe much more than I see. But no ordinary juggling trick, Master Den, will answer."

"Have I not told you who you are?" said a deep stern voice.

"Odds fish, man, you have, but you might guess that without a ghost to come and tell you, as Will Shakspere somewhere more choicely has it. In so far as you keep my secret, and are no traitor, Den, I am beholden to you, but come show your art. Can you by any possible means convince me that there is really anything in this mummery of yours, but sheer delusion made gigantic by ignorance."

"I will try."

At this moment a small trinkling sound, as if from some sweet-toned bell, sounded in the air, and the astrologer, who was no other than the famous Master Den, said at once—

"I can do so, and will upon the moment."

"Proceed, then, good familiar," said his visitor, in much the same bantering tone in which he had been speaking.

"Wouldst thou be afraid to see the arch enemy of man himself?"

"Oliver Cromwell?"

"Nay, I meant not that. Such men are but instruments after all."

Tingle—tingle went the little bell again, and then Den, after a brief pause, said—

"In truth I will not show thee aught that is evil. Thou shalt, as a proof of my power, see beauty and innocence. Thou shalt feast thine eyes for a breathing space upon one, the remembrance of who shall cling to thee as an ever present proof of the potency of my art."

"Proceed! proceed!"

"Will you solemnly promise that you will seek no further knowledge of what you here see, than your eyes may afford. Without such a promise on your sacred honour, I dare not proceed."

"I do promise on my sacred honour."

"Enough—enough."

The astrologer now threw some explosive mixture into a chafing dish where some charcoal smouldered. A loud report immediately succeeded, and then he cast in a something that produced a dense white smoke, loaded, however, by the most delicious perfumes. Jemima began to get painfully anxious to know what part she was destined to play in this pageantry, but she was soon let know. A pale crimson light began to show itself in the chamber where she was. It was well arranged by some chemical means, and then suddenly, when it was near upon its greatest intensity, the astrologer cried in a loud voice—

Spirit from the sunny south,
In thy beauty and thy truth,
Appear! Appear! Appear!

With one dash a curtain flew aside, and there was Jemima confronting the astrologer and his visitor, with the mysterious crimson light upon her, and certainly looking more like some peri than aught mortal. The stranger who was with her was a young sallow-faced man, plainly attired. He was sitting upon a large high-backed chair when this gorgeous vision burst upon his senses. For a moment he looked stunned and bewildered. Then springing to his feet, he cried—

"By the light of heaven, 'tis she."

In an instant the heavy curtain fell, and Jemima found herself once more in the absolute darkness of the room. The crimson light had vanished, and a chill sensation crept over the heart of Jemima as she shudderingly asked herself what would be the next scene of the drama in which it seemed that fate had destined her to bear a principal character. She was not, however, left long to deliberate or to speculate upon what might next occur, for the same voice that had before kept up a communication with her, sounded in her ears—

"How can we thank you for looking what you are!"

Jemima started, but almost immediately replied—

"By returning me to my route, I shall feel sufficiently repaid for playing the part you have assignd me."

"You shall be placed in safety, and indeed escorted, if it please you, to any part of the city you please to mention. Believe me, maiden, you are in the hands of those who would not willingly injure a hair of your head."

"I want no escort," said Jemima. "Place me in the street, and I shall find my way."

The hand again touched her taper fingers, and led her on through several rooms and then down a small flight of steps.

"Pardon what I am going to say, but there is sufficient evidence about your manner to convince me that you are unhappy. Is your grief such that one who would be glad to befriend you might venture to remove it?"

Jemima could have burst into tears, but she restrained herself.

"No—no—no," she said, and in another moment a door was opened and she found herself in the open street.

CHAPTER XVI

THE FATE OF THE TROOPERS.

WE now again request the attention of our readers to that house in Westminster where the twelve cavaliers were so completely beleaguered by Cromwell's troopers, as at one time to have seemed to be upon the very verge of destruction. It will be remembered that in this extremity of their fortunes, Master Waller, who resided next door, had procured the assistance of Harrison the player, who, in the disguise of an ale porter, had successfully exhibited to the dragoon, a narcotic that did its duty. We left Harrison in the room where the dragoons had lit a fire, standing in the very midst of those bulky forms, which a little harmless looking drug had for a time overcome as completely as though the fiat of some enchanter had cast a spell of slumber upon them one and all. The officer, however, had not partaken of the drugged potion. He slept, in the adjoining apartment, a natural sleep, which although noises might not disturb, accustomed as he was to the clack and din of voices, a touch from the lightest finger would awaken. However, the shed was well guarded, and that house in particular was specially under the care of Cromwell's own regiment of Ironsides. The cavaliers were, therefore, anything but out of danger, although their immediate enemies, in the shape of twelve soldiers, were for the time being put beyond the power of doing any mischief. Harrison had received instructions from Master Waller, that if he succeeded in drowning the faculties of the dragoons with the drugged ale, he was to knock six times in regular succession against the metal back of the grate, so that the cavaliers might as soon as possible avail themselves of the opportunity of breathing a somewhat purer and cooler atmosphere than they had been indulged with for the last hour or so of their incarceration in their small room of meeting. But before he gave this signal, which might be too hastily and too easily interpreted, Harrison thought it would be prudent to take some measure with regard to the officer in the adjoining room. That room did not actually open from the one in which the dragoons lay, but it opened from the same landing, the doors being only a few paces apart from each other.

"If I could lock him in now," thought Harrison, "it would be as well."

All was profoundly still in the house, and with a quiet step the player approached the door of the room in which the officer lay. It was quite dark therein, but he thought he could perceive upon the floor, wrapped in his cloak, the long figure of the horseman; he pulled the door gently close, and then, as a key was upon the outside, he turned it cautiously. The officer was a prisoner, although it would not have required any very great effort upon the part of a strong and well armed man, as he was, to break his bondage. The only chance was that he might not awaken. Of course, nothing could have been easier for Harrison to do than to take this man's life; he might have armed himself with one of the dragoons' carbines and shot him at once; or, if he preferred a less noisy mode of despatching him, there were twelve good broad swords at his disposal: he did think of it, but it was so like murder, he told himself that he could not do it. So much to the credit of Master Harrison. Having now done all that he could towards the safety of the cavaliers, he picked from the floor of the room a portion of the neck of one of the broken bottles, and with it tapped very clearly and distinctly against the back of the grate. The cavaliers had been previously informed by Waller that such would be Harrison's signal of success, and one can imagine what exquisite music to their ears those ringing tones upon the hot back of the grate were under the circumstances. Anxiety had done almost its work with them for the last half hour, which, in good truth, had appeared of frightful duration. From sitting upon the floor, so as to get into the coolest and purest stream of air, they had one and all lain down, so that, to all appearance, they remained as helpless as the dragoons who had made such havoc with the imaginary Mrs. Lightbody's ale. Those six taps upon the back of the grate, however, were as invigorating as the clangour of a war-trumpet to a charger, and they sprung to their feet heedless of the fumes of smoke into which they now elevated their heads. The grate was by far too hot to touch with their hands, but two or three of them, seizing some of the carbines that were in the room, quickly succeeded, by the use of the brass-bound butt of them, in making the grate revolve upon its centre. Oh, how delightful was the gush of cold air that came dashing into the room, cold as clear running water, or as a breeze from off a mountain's top, in comparison with the oven-like atmosphere which they had been breathing.

" Who is there ? " said Sir Walter Cardwell.

" All is right, replied Harrison, as far as I can do. Come on, gentlemen, come on."

In two minutes the twelve cavaliers were in the outer room. What long breaths of relief they each drew, and how with their handkerchiefs they dashed off the perspiration that hung like heavy beads upon their brows and faces. It was almost worth suffering what they had suffered, to feel the exquisite gratification of the relief now offered to them. There was just light enough from the smouldering wood to distinguish objects by, and there lay the twelve dragoons so still and death-like, that Lord Wilton, turning to Harrison, said—

"Of a surety you have given them a dose that will take them into the other world, good Mr. Harrison, is it not so ? "

" The dose, gentlemen," said Harrison, " was none of my mixing. I know little of such matters—it was Master Waller did that part of the business : my part was to play the porter, and I hope I have done it to your satisfaction."

" Bravely !" said Lord Sefton. " You can ask of any of us what you please at all times, Master Harrison, and, when the king has his own again, if you be not master of the players, I shall not expect to sit down in my old halls, which Cromwell has given to one of his canting generals—Ireton, I think, as the report goes."

" I shall perhaps put your lordship in mind," said Harrison, " to put his majesty in mind some day that I have this day done the state some service. But, gentlemen, the officer who commanded these troopers is in the next room."

" Ah, the officer !—and he—— "

" Certainly drunk no drugged liquor from me. He sleeps at present, and I have locked him in ; but he may awaken at any inopportune moment. What is to be done ?"

" Gentlemen," said one of the twelve, turning from Harrison, as though he, the player, had no sort of voice in the affair at all, " it is quite evident that this officer must die. This sleep that he is indulging in now must be, so far as he is concerned most unexpectedly prolonged."

" As how, my good masters ?" said Harrison, when he heard sounds of assent from the others upon the enunciation of this proposal, which to his apprehension comprehended a murder. Alas ! poor Harrison ! he himself fell a victim to what cannot be called anything but a cold-blooded assassination some months afterwards.

" Slay him as he sleeps !" said one ; " we cannot be too careful about noise, now that we are still environed by so many dangers. We can easily do it. Which is the room, Master Harrison ?—show us, and we will get rid of this bugbear, and at the same time there will be one traitor the less in England. Cromwell's officers are his main stay, and are worth the killing."

"They are indeed," said Lord Sefton.

"Gentlemen," said Harrison, as he took up one of the carbines belonging to the slumbering troopers, and stood within a pace of the door of the room, which had been partially hacked down by the soldiers to light the fire, "gentlemen, there is no time to make long speeches—so, calmly and distinctly, I implore you not to murder this sleeping man."

"Murder!—it is no murder," said Sir Walter—"this is the chance of war."

"It is murder to kill a sleeping foe. It is killing only when death occurs in fair fight."

"Pho! pho!" cried one, "we cannot entertain such scruples with these rascally tools of Cromwell. My Lord Wilton, this conduct of Master Harrison's is a leaf out of Redgrave's book."

"It is indeed."

"Stand aside, good Master Harrison; what has been said by you shall not be remembered on any other occasion to your disadvantage. Stand aside, and we will find this officer."

"No, gentlemen," said Harrison, "You shall not do this murder!"

"Shall not?"

"Such are my words, gentlemen. If any of you advance another step to do it, remember that this carbine is loaded—my finger is upon the trigger—I will fire it upon the landing, and the report will awaken the officer. He will force open the door sword in hand, and then twelve cavaliers may fall upon one man, and, if they can reconcile themselves to the act, may slay him. Come, gentlemen, this is unworthy of you all. If he should awaken, secure him, so that he cannot be mischievous, and if he should not, let him sleep on, and Heaven send him happy slumbers!"

Sir Walter Cardwell bit his lips, and then he said—

"Harrison, I don't know what to say to you; but this is no time for quarrel among the friends of King Charles the Second—be it as you wish, and may you never repent having saved such a life."

"I cannot repent," said Harrison. "It is impossible. The world is now in its breathing infancy, perchance, but when

"The cloud capped Towers. The gorgeous palaces,
The solemn temples—aye, the Great Globe itself;
With all that it inherit, shall dissolve—"

I shall not repent it. No, no. This is not one of those things that

"Babble to one of horrors on a death bed."

and now, gentlemen, will you take my advice as to a mode of escape from this miserable habitation?"

"Gladly."

"Then, without presuming upon your being very good actors, it strikes me that you might act a part that would probably ensure your safety and likewise mine. You must know that the dragoons who are guarding the street will allow any one to come to this house freely, but no one to leave it without being taken into custody, so that I am now in effect in as difficult a position as yourselves; but there are twelve of you, and here lying upon the floor are twelve military coats, helmets and boots to match as well as cloaks, swords, and carbines. Suppose you borrowed the accoutrements of these slumbering troopers for a time, and boldly marched out of the house."

"Boldly, indeed," said Lord Wilton.

"It might succeed," said Sir Walter Cardwell, "for the night is dark."

"There is one great advantage about it," said Lord Sefton, "which is, that even if we were to be suspected and stopped by the sentinels in the street, we are out of doors; and, with arms in our hands, can we not fight for our lives and liberties?"

"But what will become of you?" said Cardwell to Harrison.

"Oh, I shall trouble you to take me out with you as a seeming prisoner, which will give a great air of reality to your proceeding, as well as rescuing me."

"It truly would do so. What say you, gentlemen? Does this plan accord with your wishes?"

"Yes—yes," said they all.

"It is lucky," remarked the player, "that the change of costume can be effected with very little difficulty, for the tall boots of those troopers meet their coats, and complete the costume as far as any external observation goes. Come, gentlemen. Be quick. The stage waits."

"The stage, say you?"

"Aye, good my lord—

"All the world's a stage,
And men and women merely players."

The twelve cavaliers now, with the assistance of Harrison, proceeded to divest the troopers of their upper habiliments, and in a very short space of time, considering what then was to do, they were well disguised and all armed with the long swords and carbines, and great jack-boots and helmets, of the soldiers. Cromwell himself, at the first glance might have well believed them to form a portion of his own much vaunted and much thought of body guard."

"Gentlemen, I must leave it to your own ingenuity," said Harrison, "to imitate the long, slovenly, swinging march of the troopers. Doubtless you have often noticed them, and therefore can sufficiently play the part you have dressed, and now——"

The half-broken door of the room was opened, and the officer from the next room looked in, saying,—

"What, pray, is the meaning of all this noise and tumult upon duty?"

A death-like stillness ensued for a few moments, and then Sir Walter stepping up to the officer, said, in a stern voice,—

"Your sword sir. You are my prisoner. To resist will be madness, as you see you are most singularly outnumbered, and your soldiers lie at your feet quite unable to render you the smallest assistance."

The officer recoiled a step, but kept upon the defensive, as he gazed first upon the half-dressed man upon the floor, and then upon the seeming twelve dragoons, one of whom had addressed him in so strange a fashion. His confidence, however, soon came back to him, and fully guessing the nature of what had happened, with the one mistake, that he thought his men were killed, he said—

"If any one is weary of life, let him follow me."

He then turned abruptly and made for the stairs, intending to escape from the house, which if he had succeeded in doing, would have been fatal to the whole party.

"Now," cried Sir Walter Cardwell. "It is one life or many." He dashed after the officer, followed by two or three more with carbines. They could not overtake him, but Sir Walter stopped upon the stairs and fired at him in the passage half way to the street door.

A shriek and a heavy fall proclaimed that the shot had taken effect. The officer laid a corpse within two paces of the street door!

CHAPTER XVII.

THE GOODEN GELT.

* "Quick—quick, now," cried Harrison. "The sound of that discharged carbine will create an alarm, which your appearance in the street may quell. Leave the house, gentlemen, at once."

By this time the whole of the cavaliers had left the room, and were crowding upon the stairs, but at these words from the player, they hastily descended to the passage. They had no light, but through a rather large fan-light that was above the street-door, there came a glimmer from a lamp that was near at hand, and that was sufficient to enable them to see the officer lying upon the floor. From

EMMA PROTECTED FROM THE RUFFIANS IN THE TEMPLE BY A STRANGER

the cry he had raised, and the stillness of the body, they could have no doubt but that the shot from the carbine had proved fatal to him. Sir Walter Card-well pointed to the body, and addressing Harrison, he said—

"Do you justify us in that act, Master Harrison?"

"I do," said the player.

"On my faith and loyalty, I am glad to hear you say so, for I feared you might be of another opinion, after what you had before said of this man."

"Nay, sir, the death of this man, as it has now occurred, was a necessary measure of self-defence, and not of policy, so it is impossible any one could oppose it."

"He is right, and we were all wrong," said Lord Wilton. "You have raised yourself infinitely higher by opposing us, Master Harrison, than if you had given way to what we proposed to you. Your noble and chivalrous conduct shall not go unrewarded."

"Gentlemen—gentlemen, take me into custody and leave the house at once."

They opened the street-door, and at the moment they did so, a couple of dragoons were marching up to the house. It was a critical moment, but Sir Walter Cardwell was equal to it. He had on the dress of the sergeant of the party, and now in a gruff voice he said—

"Shoot your prisoner should he attempt to escape. March!"

The two dragoons who were the real Simon Pures stood aghast, and got out of the way, while with no very despicable imitation of what Harrison called the swinging march of the dismounted troopers, the twelve cavaliers took their way down the street. Harrison held his wrists together, as though his hands were tied, and looked as dejected as any one might be supposed to look, who, for good and special reasons, had been made a state prisoner by Cromwell's own dragoons."

"What's the meaning of that?" said one of the soldiers, who had been approaching the house. "Who was that who spoke even now?"

"Of a surety," said the other, with a strongly marked conventicle twang in his voice, "I know not; methought that the serjeant in this house was he whom the devout call "evil-speaking Johnstone," but of a surety, as I am miserable sinner, that was not Johnstone's voice."

"And yet it was the guard?"

"Aye, verily.—It looked like the guard in the flesh.—I, for one, believe that Satan may have been playing some tricks with the ungodly Johnstone. But we have both of us forgotten to ask why a carbine was found, even now within this house of suspicion."

"We have, in truth. Let's off to the guard and ask the last man. They have a prisoner with them. Who can it be, I wonder; and where is Captain Faithful? He would scarcely send away all his men and remain in the house alone. Come. We will ask them, at all events, what is the meaning of it all."

"Yea, verily, as I am strong in the arm and in the back bone, I will follow thee. Praise be to the Lord, but we may find out something."

Both the troopers thought rather more than they said to each other, for there was about the movement of the twelve seeming men-at-arms who marched down the street, a something that, to the practised eyes of the dragoons, looked suspicious. They both, at a long swinging trot, started in pursuit, their sabres and accoutrements making as much noise upon the rough uneven pavement as if a stage-coach were rattling over it.

"Hilloa!" cried one. "Stop—stop."

"Are we discovered?" whispered Sir Walter Cardwell to Lord Wilton.

"No—no. I think not. But do not stop. Sir George Moreton is in the rear, and no one can be fitter than he, with his wit and his courage, to answer any questions that may be put to him."

It was rather a nervous thing now to march on calmly under such circumstances; but the twelve cavaliers managed to do so. The dragoons overlooked the rear of the party, and one said—

"We heard a carbine fired, comrades, and the major wishes to know if ought is amiss."

"Flesh is frail," said Sir George Moreton, in a well-acted canting tone.—"Flesh is frail, and Satan has many wills.—Amen!"

"Yes, he has," said the dragoon; "and among others, my friend, now I look at you, he seems to have changed your regimental breeches from stout buff leather to silk cordovan."

"Out of the mouth of a jack-ass," said Sir George, "cometh an unmusical sound."

"That may be," said the dragoon, "but I am not such a jack-ass as not to know you are a sham trooper.—Guard!—Guard!"

He stepped back and brought his carbine to the "present" as he spoke. The cavaliers were now discovered, and there was nothing for it but to fight their way to freedom. Sir Walter cried aloud—

"Keep together, friends, until you have used your fire-arms, and then disperse. Long live King Charles!"

A rush of some half a dozen troopers was made to the support of those two who had discovered the nearly successful cheat, but the cavaliers suddenly wheeling round, faced them and fired a volley among them.

"Throw down the carbines, gentlemen," cried Sir Walter. "You have all pistols.—On—on!"

Several of the dragoons were killed by the most unexpected volley fired among them; but, with military precision, they immediately returned the fire, by which two of the cavaliers fell, and several others received wounds. They had now reached the end of the street, when two men suddenly turned the corner, followed by a trooper, with a torch. The light fell upon the two men strongly, and in them Sir Walter Cardwell recognised Cromwell and Colonel Vernon.

"A bold blow for a king!" cried Sir Walter, and he made a step forward and fired a pistol full, as he thought in Cromwell's face.

It was the sudden glance of light from the torches, or some nervousness of his own, or the wonderful good fortune of Cromwell, which had upon so many occasions befriended him, that he himself at last believed that he had a charmed life, or all combined, but the fact was most clearly apparent that the pistol bullet had missed him. In another moment Colonel Vernon had seized Sir Walter Cardwell, and they both fell to the ground struggling together.

"Fire, fire—all of you," cried Sir Walter; "do not mind me, fire upon Cromwell."

The cavaliers hesitated—there came among them another discharge of carbines; soldiers were each moment hastening to the spot, and then, as if all were suddenly seized with the same notion at the same period of time, they dispersed and fled in different directions, leaving another of their number dead, and Sir Walter a prisoner in the hands of Cromwell, and Vernon also quickly handed him over to a couple of troopers. Cromwell pointed in the direction where he had seen the last of the conspirators disappear, and immediately some of the dragoons started in pursuit. Then, turning to Vernon, he said, as camly as if nothing had happened, "we were in time, it appears, to foil these malignants."

"There is blood upon your cheek, General."

"All likely enough," said Cromwell, as he touched his cheek with his glove, and then glanced at it, "something passed me thereabout quickly. It was a pistol bullet."

"Like enough, but I have the Lord's work yet to do, Vernon, or surely these malignants would lay me low; I am mighty not in myself, but in the might that is not of this world. Let us to the house. Something strange has there happened; I would that the Lord had brought you and I here some hours before this; we are but weak instruments, after all."

It was evident that Cromwell was in one of his canting moods, either real or affected, and his most intimate acquaintance was never able, satisfactorily to themselves, to say in which. Vernon did not reply to him, and they walked on rapidly to the suspected house, followed now by about twenty soldiers, while the dead and the dying, with Cromwell's usual disregard of human life, when he had what he called a higher object in view, were passed as though they only composed the usual furnishing of the street. The house door was nearly closed, the lock had been previously completely destroyed, and now, certainly, Cromwell seemed that he either had a large amount of personal courage, or a large amount of faith in his own presumed invulnerability, for he walked a few paces in advance of the soldiers, and himself pushed open the door of the house.

"Lights!" he said, " here is some sight to see in the passage."

Flambeaux were quickly produced, and there the first object that presented itself was the dead body of the officer who had so imprudently forgotten, when he was opposed to twelve armed men, that desertion was the better part of valour.

" He has fallen in the good fight," said Cromwell; "follow me."

He at once proceeded to the room above, where the dragoons had taken up their stations, and upon entering it, he stood like a man thunderstricken, for there upon the floor lay the still perfectly insensible twelve troopers, stripped of their arms, and the upper portion of their apparel, as well as their boots. To all appearance death had swept them off, but when Cromwell saw the empty bottles lying upon the floor, and some of them still in the clinched hands of the dragoons, he smote his breast, and in a harsh strange voice he said

" Have I lived to see swine take possession of the soldiers of faith. Oh, heavy day.—Oh, heavy light. Vernon, take me hence—take me hence ; and—and—"

" Yes, General, what were you about to add ?"

" Fire, burn down, and open secret places, good Vernon. This house wants both operations ; dost comprehend me ? A gap where stands this house would look better in my eyes by to-morrow's dawn than the house itself. Dost comprehend, Vernon ? We are all in the hands of the Lord."

" I understand you, General, but may it not be attended with more danger to the surrounding buildings than you would be pleased to make them share ?"

" Eh ?"

" And likewise you would hardly wish to smother in the smoke of a conflagration those twelve troopers, whose fault, although serious, for I presume they are all drunk, scarcely deserves such an honourable fate ?"

" Ah, the night wears on apace, good Vernon. Come to me in my private apartment shortly, I have something to say to you of moment."

" I shall not fail, General, to be with you," said Vernon ; " but as regards those of the malignants, whom we might make prisoners to-night. What is your pleasure ?'

" Pleasure, good Vernon, nay, now, how strangely you miscall our thoughts and feelings. It will be pain to me to hear that you have shot them in the palace-yard ; but I expect to hear it."

Cromwell walked slowly away, and Vernon looked after him for a few moments in silence, after which he said—

" Well, I have a pleasant night's duty before me—to burn down a house, and see to some military executions, but it must be done. A fool-hardy man might trifle with a bear and her cubs, but he would need to know less of Cromwell than I do, before he would venture upon trifling with him."

In the meantime the great object of the remaining cavaliers was to get to the banks of the river, and there procure some sort of conveyance on board the Dutch ship, called the " Gooden Gelt," which was there stationed, apparently for trade, but really to aid the Royalists in their intrigues.

CHAPTER XVIII.

THE SECRET COUNCILLOR.

CROMWELL walked on gloomily until he reached the yard gate of St. James's, through which he passed, making a movement with his hand to the sentinel, which was understood to signify that the ceremony of turning out the guard was to be dispensed with, and consequently the soldier only drew himself sufficiently up and presented arms. Cromwell passed on until he reached the same apartment in which the memorable and truly appalling interview had taken place between himself and Redgrove, his secretary. The latter was in the room copying some despatches for the General, but he knew he was not wished or expected to take any notice of Cromwell's arrival, unless spoken to by him. The General threw himself upon a chair, and, turning it so that it faced a window that was in the direction of the house he had ordered to be destroyed by fire, he fixed his eyes vacantly upon the sky, no doubt expecting very shortly to see it assume the red tint that would assure him his order was fulfilled. In a quiet earnest sort of way Redgrove did at times look towards Cromwell, and he was rather surprised that nothing was said to him. After a time, however, Cromwell gave a sort of grunt of seeming satisfaction, and turned away from the window, saying—

"Redgrove, I have for you a confidential mission."

"I shall endeavour, sir, to execute it becomingly," said Redgrove, and then, as he looked up from his writing, he saw that the sky, through the window, bore the tint of fire, and he rose, exclaiming as he did so—

"Sir, there is a fire."

"Let it burn, Redgrove."

"Then, sir, you know of it? It flames fiercely enough, and must be near at hand ; will it not be prudent to do——"

"Nothing, Redgrove. Let the fire burn, It is purposely lit to warm some persons, so let it burn, and attend to me. I am about to make a confidence with you, Redgrove—a domestic not a political confidence. Remember, I am now speaking to you not as a general, not as an employer, but as a private friend. Will you accord to me that title?"

"I am much honoured, sir, by it."

"Well, then, you know my poor son Richard?"

Redgrove inclined his head, and Cromwell continued, in a voice of grief—

"Alas! he is weak of body and infirm of purpose. Yes, he is most infirm of purpose, and yet this nation looks and must look—— Well, well, no matter ! I am wandering from the subject. Redgrove, I have another sore—Richard's elder brother, of whom the world knows nothing—but I, alas, too much."

"An elder son than Richard, sir ! Indeed, the world knows nothing of such a son. Perhaps he will hold a better place in these stormy times ?"

"Redgrove, that other son of mine is—I am his father, and loved him—perhaps love him still, and yet I say it—he is a villain !"

Redgrove started.

"I am accustomed," said Cromwell, "when speaking to such men as you to speak clearly, and to call things by their right names, using language that comes closest and nearest to the meaning meant to be expressed, therefore say I that Harry Cromwell is a villain. These eyes have not beheld him now for eight long years. It is needless that I should detail to you the amount of his pride and worthlessness, but there came a day at last when—when I received from him a blow !"

"A blow !"

"Aye, Redgrove. You are childless. May the great God keep you so ! He had many times struck my spirit, but there came a day upon which I refused to rapacity and threats that which they required for the purposes of wild folly, and I received from the hands of my own child a blow. Oh ! Redgrove, I can feel it yet—I shall ever feel it. To the grave it will go with me !"

Cromwell shook as if some sudden convulsion had come over him, and Redgrove would fain have said something consolatory to him, but he felt that all ordinary topics of sympathetic speech would be but a mockery of what Cromwell must at that moment feel, and he was judiciously silent. In a few moments the general was more composed.

"That erring son," he said, " is now about the age of twenty-six, and this is his last missive to me, as well as the first I have had from him since his departure from England, eight years since. Read it, Redgrove, your full knowledge of its contents will spare me some speech."

Redgrove read a crumpled up piece of paper that Cromwell laid before him, and upon it were these words :—

"Harry Cromwell requires supplies for his good estate. Will he be Prince if the crown of England fits your brows? In the meantime, fifty pieces if you hate me, and one hundred if you love me ; so no more from your Prince to be,

"HARRY CROMWELL, at the St. Barnabus's Head, in Ludgate."

"What think you of such a missive?" said Cromwell. "Speak, Redgrove—no—no, say nothing. I can see what you feel. There is gold. Take it to this godless man, and bid him name his price to breathe the air of another land than this. Go—go at once, good Redgrove, and when your mission is performed forget, Harry Cromwell."

Redgrove took the money, and bowing, left the apartment ; for he knew that prompt obedience to his mandates was a much more estimable quality with Cromwell than any speeches. In five minutes' time he was on his way to Ludgate with the gold, which he found to be seventy-five pieces—a strange compromise between the sum that was to proclaim "hate," and the sum that was to speak to the bad son of "love." While Redgrove and Cromwell were thus employed, a dreadful scene was taking place at the house where the troopers still slept from the effects of the drugged ale that they had so imprudently partaken of, and which had so completely plunged their senses in forgetfulness. Colonel Vernon set about executing the orders of Cromwell. But he did not construe those orders to go so far as to prevent him from warning the parties upon each side of the doomed habitation of the danger they might run, and devising with them means of rendering it less hazardous than otherwise it might be. He knocked hastily at the house of Master Waller, whose share in the plots of the cavaliers was very far from being at all suspected by Cromwell or his officers. Indeed, they took Waller to be quite the other way in thinking. This was anything but a welcome summons to Waller, who saw from out of his windows that it was from an officer with a strong party of dragoons, but he knew that while everything might be gained by coolness and ease, nothing could be gained by any show of fear. He opened the door at once, himself, and cordially greeted Vernon, who said—

"Master Waller, the general has ordered the next house to be gutted by fire, and I merely wish to tell you that I will see it done with as much regard to the safety of your house as possible."

"I am much beholden to you. Did you find the malignants?"

"Not wholly. The expedition may be called a failure. We have a prisoner though.—One Sir Walter Cardwell, and some three or four, I think, have fallen from the fire of the soldiers."

"The Lord be good to us all!" said Waller. "May a just cause, which is for the happiness of England, in my humble estimation, triumph in the fulness of time. I thank you for your courtesy, colonel."

Vernon ordered the windows to be thrown open, for he fully expected, as he and Cromwell both thought, that the intoxicated dragoons would be roused up and make their escape when they began to be singed a little, and a singeing they amply deserved, even in the milder affectation of Colonel Vernon, who shrunk from their destruction. He considered he should be sufficiently carrying out the orders of Cromwell by sending a sheet of flame through the house, and stopping short of burning it down, which might endanger the neighbourhood ; for who shall quell the spirit of fire when once invoked? To the military commanders of that period, the setting fire to a house was never a matter of much difficulty. A few trusses of straw were purchased from a neighbouring stable, and then cast at the foot of the stairs, after which the ceremony concluded by a soldier throwing a link amid the combustible mass. A light flame arose, waving and sweeping up the staircase, and laying hold of every piece of dry wood-work it met with. Dense volumes of smoke began to make their way out of the top windows, and Colonel Vernon, who stood upon the steps of the house opposite, muttered to himself—

"Are the fools indeed so far gone in liquor, that they will allow themselves really to be burnt?"

This seemed indeed to be the fate of the troopers, whether Cromwell really meant it or not, for no one stirred. Had the smallest suspicion of the real state of the case crossed the mind of Vernon, he would have taken active measures to rescue the dragoons; but no one held drunkenness in greater abhorrence than he; and when finally a portion of the roof of the house fell in, and the flames began to subside, in consequence of the extreme dampness of the timbers of the house, from being unoccupied, he stamped with rage, as he cried—

"Their deaths be upon their own heads! The fools! Cromwell even may think this going a little too far, when he hears the result; but I have obeyed orders, at all events, and I cannot help it."

He still lingered for a short time about the spot. The fire was smothered, and only dull wreaths of smoke ascended from the ruins of the house. The alarm of the neighbours was subsiding, and the idlers who had been drawn to the street, but checked from approaching the fire by strong patrols of dismounted dragoons, dispersed upon finding that all was over.

"Call in the sentinels," said Vernon to a subordinate.

The bugle was sounded, and in a few moments the soldiery in one compact body left the spot; and that was all that took place just then connected with what was somewhat pompously called the "Abingdon Street Plot," and which was made use of by Cromwell within the next few weeks as an excuse for some extremely disagreeable domicilliary visits to the estates and mansions of several noblemen, who were suspected of being favourable to the Royal cause. Colonel Vernon marched his men to the barrack-rooms, adjoining what is called the Colour Court of St. James's Palace. The events of that night were not got over, for the orders of Cromwell regarding Sir Walter Cardwell had yet to be executed. This unfortunate nobleman had needlessly committed himself by calling out, "Long live King Charles!" upon the occasion of the *fracas*, for it could not be called much more, in Abingdon Street, and consequently had brought himself within the summary provisions of an order in council, that condemned to death any one uttering such cries. Probably, however, if he had not said what he did say, some other mode would have been found of summarily convicting him, for certain it is, that Cromwell, who knew the courage, the resources, and the energy of Sir Walter, had determined upon his execution the moment he heard he was captured. There was but one who might have interfered with a chance of success. That one was the Secretary Redgrove, and he had gone to Ludgate.

CHAPTER XIX.

THE EXECUTION.

SIR WALTER was imprisoned in a small room which still exists. If the stranger who may be anxious to see this room will walk through the principal gateway of St. James's Palace, and then pass under an arched way on the right from the Colour Court, and then turn to the left, he will find himself in a quiet ancient part of the building, and he will see not far from where a sentinel holds a somewhat lonely watch, a row of three windows with bars. The centre one of those windows communicated with Sir Walter Cardwell's brief prison, for he was not there more than two hours. Between that cloister-looking covered way, upon one side of the Colour Court, and the spot now occupied by the building that was intended as a palace for the Duke of York, was a large irregular space, from which the Green Park could be easily reached, and close to that space were the stables of Cromwell's regiment of dragoons. Sir Walter had no suspicion of the rapid manner in which he was to be sent to his execution; and he was pacing his prison, thinking of what probable questions would be put to him on the morrow, when he fully expected he would have to undergo an examination before Cromwell, and those whom he called his council. Suddenly these cogitations were interrupted by the door opening, and the appearance of a guard of dismounted dragoons, headed by an officer, who merely said—

"You will follow us, Sir Walter Cardwell."

"Humph!" said Sir Walter. "I shall be examined, then, to-night, I presume. Well—well, be it so. I demand honourable treatment, and the respect due to my rank. I am a baronet of this kingdom.'

The officer made no reply, but marched at the head of his men, among whom came the prisoner, upon whom a strict and a wary eye was kept by those nearest to him. In this manner, two of the soldiers, bearing links, proceeded to the space which we have spoken of, and slightly described.

"Halt!" cried the officer.

The soldiers paused, and one stuck his link in the ground, upon a spot which was indicated by the officer; and no sooner was that done, than a person in half-civil half-military costume advanced with a paper in his hand. Sir Walter looked at these proceedings with surprise, not unmixed with grave suspicions as to the tendency of them. He had before heard of rapid military executions upon that spot, and yet he could hardly think that a man of his standing and consideration could be cut off in so summary a way.—He did not know Cromwell very well! The mongrel-looking personage with the paper in his hand motioned to one of the dragoons to hold him the other link, so that he could read by it; and then, in a rapid official tone, which means an unintelligible one, he gabbled over a kind of proclamation, which condemned to present death, according to military law, all persons found in arms against the state, and at the same time uttering seditious cries. At the conclusion of the hearing, he said—

"Sir Walter Cardwell, have you anything to say why the penalty you have knowingly incurred should not be carried into effect?"

"This is monstrous!" cried Sir Walter. "I demand a fair hearing!"

"You are having one. Have you anything to state?"

"Much; and I demand an interview with General Cromwell."

"Which is not granted.—Anything else?"

"I—I—Oh! but this is murder. If I have done wrong, let me be tried by those who can and may show that they have a right to try me; but if you take my life now, it is, and can be nothing else but murder!"

"You protest, then, against it?"

"Most assuredly I do."

"Very well, Sir Walter Cardwell, your protest against the proceedings will be duly recorded, I assure you; and now my duty is over, I sincerely lament that you have thought proper, with a full knowledge of the law, to place yourself in so awful a position.—There is your warrant, sir (to the officer). It will be my business, from a distance, to see the execution done."

"But I had no knowledge of this law," cried Sir Walter.

"It's an axiom in law," said the other, "that all men know the laws of the state under the government of which they live. I have the honour to bid you good night."

The official personage walked away, and was lost in the shadow of the arched-way, from which he could see the execution. The officer approached Sir Walter, and said—

"You will stand or kneel, as you please, by this link. It is better the soldiers should see you clearly, than run the hazard of only wounding you."

Sir Walter Cardwell drew his breath short and thick. He had faced death upon the battle field, and he had fought a duel or two; but to be butchered in this manner with a hideous mockery of legality about it, was a ten times worse fate than ever he had pictured to himself as possible to overtake him. It would have been better to have fallen in a struggle with the dragoons, in or out of the house in Abingdon Street. Better to have died in any way, so that he had arms in he hand, and his blood was warm; but now, in all the coolness of inaction, to be brought out to be slaughtered by the flickering light of a penny link.—It was more than the bravest could look upon with anything in the, shape of calmness.—It was death without excitement—anger—applause or glory.—It was horrible—most horrible.   He stood by the link that had been stuck in the damp ground, looking about him with his ghastly face, and his eyes half starting from their sockets, as though he expected that at the last moment some unexpected aid would come to him.

JEMIMA'S DANGER IN THE ABBEY.

"Right face!" cried the officer, when six of the dragoons had got about twelve paces from the doomed man.   "Make ready!"

"Hold!" cried Sir Walter Cardwell, as he faced them, 'and folded his arms upon his breast.   "This is murder; but I am a cavalier, and will show you how a soldier and a gentleman can die by the hands of a king's assassins and a nation's tyrants.—Long live King Charles the second!"

"Present!—Fire!"

A rattling discharge of the six carbines followed; but there for a moment stood Sir Walter Cardwell.—Then he fell forward upon his face like a lump of lead.

Recover arms!—Left face!—March!"

The dragoons were marched to their quarters—a rough shell was brought, into which the dead body was thrown, and that night it found a grave in St. Margaret's Church-yard, by the side of many others whom the stern policy of Cromwell found, or thought, it necessary to lay in the cold earth, where the weary are at rest, and where counts and kings are but the empty baubles of a fool. Cromwell was alone, without a light, when the rattling discharge of the carbines fell upon his ears.— He sprang to his feet as though each bullet had found a resting place from its hot hissing flight in his own heart.

"A light!—A light!—Lights!" he called, in a voice that so startled the attendants, who were in an adjoining room, that they one and all rushed in without any ceremony, fearful that some assassin had found his way to the general, and was completing his purpose. They found Cromwell with his hair disordered, and his eyes half starting, while his lips quivered with emotion. "Lights!—Lights!" he added. "Did I not order lights? I—I thought I had long since ordered lights. I am not well!"

"Shall we send for Master Wells, the physician, or——"

"No. The Lord will be physician to those who are doing his work. I grieve for men of sin, and for a land, which ever, like the cities of the plain, is full of abomination. I wrestle with the evil one. Begone. Interrupt me not. I stand upon the mount. Begone, I say. The Lord is with me."

The attendants lit some half-dozen wax candles, and then quietly withdrew. They were not at all unaccustomed to find some period of excitement in their master turned off into a pretended fit of religious enthusiasm. When Cromwell was alone he placed his hands behind his back, and paced the room.

"Another!" he said, "another! aye, and there must be many more ere this land is free from the halo of king-craft. How old prejudices cling to folk, like old disorders. The plague spot, which fools call loyalty, descends from father to son, in England, as though it were of a piece with other possessions.—Loyalty! What is loyalty? An adherence to a system, or to a man, or to a woman? Loyalty! It must be the sort of submission which fools give to knaves.—Truly the worship of idols has not departed from this land, nor will it, I much fear, unless it be washed away in blood. Well, there is one foe the less to-night. The fall of Cardwell will discomfit many sleek loyalists in London.—That man was in himself a walking plot. Ha! Who knocks?"

The door opened, and the mysterious man in grey stood upon the threshold. Cromwell cowered before him, and shrunk into a seat. The strange visitant closed the door, and approached three steps into the room, and then paused. This singular being merits some description of a more particular character than we were before able to give of him. It was not his grey clothing, of such a strange and universal colour, that gave the horrible singularity to his appearance, but it was his grey face and his grey hands! There was no colour of flesh about him.—His face without variations, was of a horrible, bluish, sickly grey, and the appearance the colour gave to his eyes, which were bright and restless, was most preternatural. His appearance was sufficient to strike the strongest minded with a shuddering horror.

"Again!" gasped Cromwell, "again!"

"Yes," said a deep, strange voice, that sounded as though it were some clear artificial imitation only of human sounds. "Yes, I am here again. The hour is coming."

"No—no—no.—Not yet,—when?—when?"

"Would you have me name to you the minute, Cromwell?"

"No—and yet—I—would gladly know. Have I a foe near me? Tell me that. Have I a foe near me? Must I suspect even those who are garnered up as precious things in my heart? Mysterious being! You, who from your rare knowledge of the past, have taught me to believe you can forsee the future— tell me, I say, whom and what I have most to fear?"

"I have before spoken. I only come now to warn you that time is speeding, and yet as I have advised, I will advise again. You have told all, I am your secret councillor. Hast anything now to ask of me?"

"No—no—no."

"What! no enterprise on foot?"

"None. The plot which I told you I was seeking to discover the authors of, is, I think, broken up, although I failed in—as I expected and hoped—seizing upon the conspirators."

"I warned you that there would be a mixed success. Where is your informer!"

"The man, Adams?"

"Aye."

"He is safe from the vengeance of the cavaliers; who will, of course, attribute their discomfiture to him. He is at lodgings in Whitehall, and only will stir out for a time, with the owls. He has had his reward, and yet he is marvellously fearful."

"Let him leave the country. There is a Dutch vessel named the Gooden Gelt lying in the river. You suspected it of harbouring Royalists. You were wrong. It had nothing but a secret mercantile character. Let him go on board. She will sail in three days, and the captain, for money, will secrete him."

"He shall be advised. But tell me; is there no fate for me but a dreadful death? The—gibbet? Oh no—no!"

"Aye, the gibbet. But the wood that is to erect it, grows yet in the forest. Farewell, Cromwell, farewell!"

The grey man opened the door, and was about to leave the chamber, when he confronted Colonel Vernon exactly upon the threshold. One could not pass for the other. Vernon placed his hand upon his sword, but Cromwell cried with a loud voice of mingled fear and anger—

"No—no—no. For your soul's safety's sake, hinder him not, Vernon. Hush—hush—hush. Let it pass—pass——"

Vernon, in the surprise of the moment, slipped aside, and the grey man glided noiselessly away, and was soon lost to sight in the gloom of the corridor.

"Gracious Heaven! my good general, what is the meaning of this?"

"Hush—hush!"

Vernon had never looked, and never in sober truth felt so utterly astonished in all his life, as by this most mysterious conduct on the part of Cromwell. To see that man of iron nerves so completely subdued and trembling at what seemed to be a something that a man of firm purpose would have resolved upon fully ascribing, was a spectacle that he, Vernon, was in truth most unprovided against. No wonder, then, that he continued to gaze at Cromwell as if he himself were an apparition.

"Vernon," at length said the general, "you have seen the bane of my existence. Yon most mysterious figure, which has just left us, comes to me at strange times, and by telling me of the past, makes me believe, in spite of my judgment, in its predictions of the future. This is the secret that has always trembled on my lips in my interviews with you. This is the conversation that I promised you."

"But how gets he admittance?"

"By my orders, and yet I think he is no being of this world; and were I to trebly bar my doors against him, he would find his way; but say no more to me of this to-night, Vernon, for in very truth I am sick at my soul. Let us talk of other matters, my good Vernon. At some other juncture we will renew this solemn and most strange subject of discourse."

CHAPTER XX.

ROYALTY AFLOAT.

VERNON could have said that the present subject was the most interesting that he had, heard of for some time, but he did not like, in defiance of the command of Cromwell, to renew it, and he therefore made some casual remarks upon other topics, and the conversation soon took a political turn. The conference lasted more than an hour, and at the end of it, Vernon said, as if in a careless manner—

"I presume, general, that your mysterious friend in grey makes his visits with tolerable regularity?"

Cromwell's countenance assumed a deadly tinge, as he said—

"How mean you?"

"I mean that he comes at regular intervals, and at regular hours, doubtless?"

"No. He seldom names a time for his reappearance, although upon this visit he has said that he will be here again this night week, at six o'clock, which will be one hour after sunset."

"Well, one must bear with visitations from the other world in the best way we may, and as the being is such, of course, any resistance to his presence would be as foolish as it would be futile."

Cromwell made an impatient gesture with his hand, as though he deprecated all further discussion upon such a subject, and Vernon, who knew that the temper of the general was not one that should be tried too far, at once gave the conversation up for the present. At least, so far as regarded any conversation with Cromwell, he did, but as for himself, he made up his mind to a different course, for he muttered, as he paced through the gorgeous apartments that led from the room of the general—

"This must not be. Higher consequences may result from this affair than merely awakening the superstition of Cromwell. He must not, and shall not, be shackled by such a bugbear as this, who may, after all, be an emissary merely of the cavaliers. Had I not seen this of Cromwell, by my faith, I could not have believed it, if an angel from heaven had come and told me of it."

But Colonel Vernon was not in a position to judge of the means by which this grey man, whether he were mortal or not, had obtained his great influence over the mind of Cromwell. Those means consisted of such ample information concerning the early life and private family affairs of the general, that he could not conceive it possible any one could know them except from supernatural sources. There were some things told him by that man which he fully believed were locked up in the deepest recesses of his own heart. It was under these circumstances, then, that Cromwell lent an ear to predictions of the future, the remembrance of which frequently staggered his judgment, paralysed his courage, and made him shrink appalled from enterprises that otherwise he would have carried out with his usual pertinacity and energy. Events, however, are hurrying on which will soon proclaim who and what this mysterious visitor of Cromwell is; but, in the meantime, we must transfer our attention to a very different scene to what was enacting in the palace of St. James's. The reader has, doubtless, not forgotten the Gooden Gelt, a Dutch trading vessel which lay in the river, ostensibly for mercantile purposes, but really for the purpose of affording a sudden asylum to any of the cavalier party in London or its suburbs, whose failure in any notable plot might have the effect of making their absence a necessary adjunct to their existence. Cromwell had his suspicions of this vessel, and had once searched it. But he did not choose that those connected with the ship should know the full extent of those suspicions, for he hoped that at some lucky moment, by suddenly pouncing upon her, he should make some prisoners of importance. He had, therefore, affected to be satisfied when he had searched the Gooden Gelt upon the occasion of his visit to Walk-in-the-right-path Strangeway's house, where he hoped to find Charles the Second. Indeed Cromwell, with a duplicity that he not unfrequently exercised, and which he no doubt thought fair enough in war, had given the captain of the Gooden Gelt a certificate that he was in the river upon "good purposes," and was not to be molested lightly or upon vague suspicions. We need not say that the value of this document was duly estimated by the Dutch skipper, who lighted a prodigious pipe with it, and ordered a better watch than ever to be kept on board the vessel. Things were in this state on board the Gooden Gelt when the serious affray upon the river had taken place between Sir Charles Courtney and the Puritans, who would, without any compunctions of conscience, have taken the lives of him and his young and beautiful bride but for the interposition of the King himself, in the well manned and well armed boat that came to the rescue, when all hope seemed to be quite extinguished. The boat which conveyed Charles and his friends, including Sir Charles Courtney and his bride, at first made way swiftly for the Gooden Gelt, but the result of a brief consultation was, that it would be imprudent to do so, now that Sir Charles Courtney, an object of present popular exasperation, was seen from the shore to have been received by them. Accordingly, the boat was pulled to a little landing place upon the opposite side of the river, called the "Shallow," and there the whole party landed. The scheme was to disperse for about half an hour, and then to come down in two or three parties, and to take separate boats to get on board the Gooden Gelt, without exciting so much observation as when they all went together. This succeeded the better, inasmuch as there were several watermen on both sides of the river, regularly in the pay of the Royalists, who, at a signal, always tendered their services, and were accepted as a matter of course upon giving a countersign. We will suppose, then, that the whole of the parties in the boat have by twos and threes found their way to the Gooden Gelt, and we will now beg the reader to descend with us the companion hatchway, and to mind not to break his head against the top of the door frame, and then to enter the not very salubrious *state* cabin—they call things by strange names on shipboard—of the Gooden Gelt. The appointments are of a rough order, but there is now an evident desire to give the affair a respectable look. The table is cleanly wiped down—an arm-chair is placed at the upper end of it, while other seats, of rather a heterogeneous character, are ranged upon each side. The arm-chair is occupied by Charles the Second that was to be, but then the fugitive with three thousand pounds fine upon his head, as a "public destructive of the peace of the nation." The seats on each side of the table were filled by some of the principal and most young and daring of those who had staked their all upon the probabilities of a restoration, which, after all, none of their plots succeeded in producing, but which, as all the world knows, was eventually brought about by the treachery of Monk, and the stupidity of his troops. This meeting, then, on board the Gooden Gelt, was in effect a council of state between Charles and his then cabinet ministers, at which he himself presided.

"Well, gentlemen," said Charles, who had his hat on, the rest being uncovered. "have you any news for us of a fresher date than the last, which came up to the evening of the 6th, I take it?"

"There is a messenger, sir," said one, "on board, who brings papers and letters."

"Ah! papers and—and letters. Give me the letters."

A small packet was handed to the King, and he looked this eagerly over, until he selected one which he broke the seal of, and read with great eagerness. This letter was addressed as follows—"To Master Morton, these, God willing."

The countenance of Charles darkened as he read the letter, and with a peculiar exclamation he thrust it into his pocket, and commenced half angrily drawing with his finger nails upon the arm of the chair in which he sat. For a short time the council was silent, but the Lord Guilford spoke boldly, saying—

"Sire, if you have received gloomy intelligence, it is fit and proper that we, of your council, with our lives all hanging by a thread, should know of it."

"Tush, man! They are notes of private affairs, and concern not the state."

As Charles spoke, he took a handkerchief from his pocket, and wiped his face with it ; and in so doing he pulled forth the letter, and it fell to the ground. Lord Guilford saw it fall, and so did others ; but the king did not ; they let it lie where it was, for they really wished to see what it contained. They had all too much at stake to be very particular how they got information which might guide them free of danger, in such amazingly critical times as those in which they lived.

"Well, gentlemen," added Charles, "is anything to be proposed ?"

"Your majesty," said the Earl of Guilford, "is aware of the advice Sir Walter Cardwell gave in his letter. He likewise stated that he would propose as much to the twelve gentlemen who held the meetings in London in your service."

"Aye! An armed insurrection !"

"Just so, sire ; but so well-timed that it was hoped it could not well fail if your majesty would give it that degree of moral force which your presence could not fail to impart to it."

"And when did I ever shrink, gentlemen ?"

"Never, your majesty ; nor did my speech go the length of intimating so much."

"I cry you mercy, my lord, I thought it did. But come"——And here Charles assumed that manner, which people who translate everything favourably for kings, called fascinating. "Come, my good lords and friends, we must not quarrel about trifles. Decide that I am to pluck Cromwell by the beard in Whitehall, and I will do it, rather than that merry England should groan under that worst of tyrannies, the tyranny of religious cant."

"Ah, sire, no one will advise you to endanger overmuch your precious life, which is of such importance to us. The proposition was, that from different quarters of the city, bands of armed men should start ,picking up as they infallably would do, many dissipated stragglers upon the way, and concentrate their force at Charing-cross, where, should the affair bear a good front, and a lively expectation, your majesty, from some adherent's house, should make your royal appearance, and head the movement."

"This plan," said one, "if it had no other recommendation, has at least that of such exceeding boldness, that it ought to succeed."

"Well, gentlemen," said Charles, "are you all decided upon this ?"

"We are, your majesty, with the exception of one point."

"And what is that ?"

"We all naturally shrink from advising you, sire, to run the risk of the enterterprise. Then do we feel that never had councillors so difficult a task before them, for while we know the vast importance of the king's person as a rallying point, we likewise know that to lose you would be to lose England."

"Well," said Charles, "I, too, have given this matter some thoughts, and the result is, my fair conviction is, that it is only my presence at Charing-cross that will impart to this bold plan that power and substance without which it would fail. Odd's fish, when the folks who are assembling see me there, they will say to themselves, "There must be something in this affair, for Charles would not put his head into the lion's mouth exactly."

"Then your majesty decides——"

"In favour of the enterprise, my lords, and let it be carried out as soon as all prudence will allow it."

"Then there is hope for England !"

Charles rose and bowed slightly, which was a signal that the council was broken up; and then he said—"All details of this matter we leave to your better judgment, gentlemen, and in the meantime we think we had better go to Denny's house again until things are ripe. By the bye, one point is of great importance, and that is, where we shall find refuge until the moment arrives when we are to make our appearance as becomes us."

"There is a house, sir, kept solely by a young man named Alfred Beaumont, some half way between Oxford-street and Charing-cross : we can all pledge ourselves for his fidelity."

"Alfred ——"

"Beaumont, your majesty."

"Humph! Where have I heard the name of Alfred lately ? I cannot call to mind ; but it is no matter, there are more Alfreds than one in the world. My lords, we bid you good day, and all happiness. Sir Charles Courtney, where have you bestowed the Puritan's lovely daughter ?"

"In safety, sire."

"Oh, very good—ah—hem. You are a very fortunate man, Sir Charles, indeed. In safety—quite right."

CHAPTER XXI.

A LOVE LETTER.

From public affairs, and the deliberations of princes and lords, although those deliberations were conducted in so undignified a region as the cabin of the Gooden Gelt, we must turn to better, although more homely themes, pausing only to look at the letter which the frivolous in youth, and vicious in age, Charles II., left upon the cabin floor, and which Lord Guilford had kept his eye upon.

"My Lords," he said, when Charles was gone, "the king has dropped a letter, and as these are not, by any means—

"Piping times of peace ; "

in which people can play with state affairs, and not feel that they are touching edged tools, it behoves us to have all the information we can, so I shall take the liberty of reading his majesty's letter."

The council assented, thereby proving how little real respect they had for Charles, and how much of a mere puppet they considered him in the hands of a party ; a sort of banner, waving as a rallying point, but being of itself of no intrinsic value. The letter, as enunciated by Lord Guilford, was as follows :—

"Harry Morton,—You say you love me. Oh ! what am I to think of that love which would destroy all virtue, and make me despicable, in my own eyes, as well as in the eyes of all who love what is good ? No, I cannot, will not meet you, or fly with you on board the Dutch ship, as you propose. My husband returns to-morrow. If I meet him with sadness upon my brow, I will at least meet him with innocence at my heart. It is true I am young, and know little of the world, but I suspect you are not what you seem, and that your secret principally is, that you do not mean me well ; so farewell for ever.—Annie Lucombe."

The members of the council looked at each other in silence for some few moments, and then Lord Guilford said—

"It seems, gentlemen, that we have only hit upon a little disappointment of royalty, it is to be hoped that this Annie is some Puritan's wife."

"Very likely." said another. "But we must not judge harshly of his majesty. Perhaps after profound reflection, he has hit upon the expedient of seducing their wives, as the mode of confounding the intellects of Cromwell's adherents."

A general laugh succeeded this sally ; and we shall now leave the Golden Gelt, in order to transcribe another letter, which was left at Mr. Dashall's, the mercer, in the Strand, for Jemima. Of course it came from her forsaken Alfred, and of course she declared she would not read it, and of course she read every word of it. It ran thus,—

"My Jemima,—May I still call you my Jemima ? Dare I still address you by such an appellation ? Yes, yes, you will be mine own, even should you r cruelty drive me far, far from you. Jemima, I am upon my trial. I am found possessed of your love. How came I by it? Was it not by your own free gift? Yes. Your own heart will answer yes to that question. I have lost your love. Why? It is for you to answer that Jemima. I want that answer, and do you know, Jemima, one of the things that made me love you, was your love of truth, and that strong principle of *right*, which I saw, or fancied I saw, in your composition. There is a service to-night in the abbey. I shall be there. Come, and I will be near you. Remain away, and refuse the explanation I now for the last time ask, and you will never see me more.—P. S. My Jemima, come to me—ALFRED BEAUMONT."

"I will," said Jemima. It was the postscript that decided. There was truth in the letter, and tenderness in the postscript, but as tenderness and feelings are in this world long odds against truth and justice, it is doubtful if the rather stern and reasonable epistle would have sufficed to make Jemima do what was right, if the postscript had not contained, in few words, a world of sad and beautiful persuasion.

"Yes!" said she. "In time to come, I will not have it upon my mind to say that I quarrelled with the being I loved best upon earth, without a full and free explanation. I will go to the abbey, and may God, whose house of prayer that is, sanctify our meeting! It will be for joy, or for sorrow."

From the moment of making up her mind to proceed to the old abbey, Jemima could think of nothing else, and as we do not intend to relate anything else, until we have got through with her interview with her lover, and another personage whom she there met, we will assume that it is the hour of eight, and that the poor girl is upon the threshold of the old—then old Abbey, of Westminster. She had been conscious as she passed down Whitehall, of some one at times treading close upon her heels and once she had turned, when a voice exclaimed—

"By Heavens, 'tis she!"

The voice was quite unknown to Jemima, as well as the person of the man who uttered the exclamation, and she quickened her pace accordingly, but, as she passed into the abbey, she became, by a side glance, quite aware that the stranger had entered the sacred edifice along with her. Now, Alfred had not mentioned in his note any particular spot where he would be found, so that Jemima paused by a little oratory within, within which were the effigies of some mail-clad warriors, piously disposed, with their ancles crossed, to denote that they had formed a portion of the host of fools and fanatics who made up the great Crusade. Paying but little attention to these memorials of departed chivalry, Jemima waited anxiously the arrival of Alfred, but before he came voice close to her, said—

"Do you know the gentleman who came in with you? Remember, you are in my custody."

Jemima started, and upon glancing round, she saw a person in the habit of some official, which habit was a kind of mixture of the clothing of the reign of the first Charles, with a penitential looking jerkin and hat.

"What do you mean?" she said.

"Hush," replied the man—"he comes. Say but a word that is displeasing to me, and your head and his may both pay the forfeit. Engage him in conversation, that I may listen to his voice."

The same stranger who had spoken to Jemima in Whitehall, now came up to her, and partially hiding his face with his hat, he said—

"Throughout how many streets of London can such transcendant beauty venture to travel alone? Ah! fair one! are you born for mischief or for joy?"

There was a libertineness about the style of this speech that Jemima was far from liking, and she drew back, saying—

"I do not know you, sir."

"Ah!" he replied, "I would that I could plead equal ignorance. Do you not at times shed the light of your beauty upon the house of Master Dashall, in the Strand?"

"Sir," said Jemima, "I neither know you, nor wish to know you; but in simple charity I tell you that you are watched, and one here present has told me that your head is in danger."

"Odds fish! did he? But—but—who is Alfred?"

"Who?"

KING CHARLES THE SECOND.

"Humph! I really think we are all at cross purposes in some way. Oh! is that an acquaintance of yours?"

A young cavalier hurried up to Jemima, and she, the moment she saw him, said—

"Alfred Beaumont, for my sake, get into no quarrel here; but if you will walk homeward with me, I will speak with you."

No. 11.

"You see, Alfred," said the insolent stranger, "how careful the young lady is of your safety. You are a favoured suitor, it seems—a fool of fortune."

"Sir!"

"Oh, don't bluster! I never brawl in a church, not I. But we shall meet elsewhere, when I will make you eat my dagger here, if you will not, as the wiser alternative by far, forego all hope, or right, or title to the ghost of a smile from this fair one, who is a world too good for you."

"Insolence!"

"Oh, no—not at all—not at all! Were I really disposed to anger you, I could say things that would make you roar again."

"I will make you roar again ere I have done with you," said Alfred, as he made a step towards his vexatious companion.

"Follow me, then, out at the door there, by Poet's Corner, and I will soon show you who is best master of fence. Come, if you dare to follow me."

Alfred rushed after his foe, who went with a swift pace. Jemima followed, and so did the official person who had spoken to her. He gained upon her, saying—

"Keep them engaged; you shall have a hundred—two hundred pounds—you shall indeed, if I take that man prisoner—I know him!"

"Alfred?"

"No; the other. It is Charles!—the King!—that would be. I was a servant with his father. Stop him!"

Jemima was thunderstricken at this intelligence; and the slight pause she made to listen to the spy, enabled Alfred and the king to get on a little in advance, when the former suddenly turning, said—

"Hush, Alfred Beaumont, do you know Lord Guilford?"

"Lord Guilford? I—I—yes."

"Then we ought to be mutual friends, since we both know him. I only quarrelled with you to draw you away."

"Who are you, then?"

"Why, if I were to write my name as I wish, it should be Charles Rex."

"The king! Oh, my liege! I——"

"Hush! Look at that fellow. He has been dogging me, and by some strange and damnable fatality my enemies know me through disguise, although my friends do not. See, he comes, and already thinks himself king-catcher to the Commonwealth of England. Ha! he comes nobly on. The sword dazzles him."

"I will dazzle him," said Alfred.

They had reached nearly to the little door in the wall of the cathedral that leads into the open space from Poet's Corner, and then, when they turned, they saw plainly, for no one else was there, the man trying to force his way past Jemima, who held him by the lappet of his coat. Before Charles or Alfred Beaumont could reach him, the rascal raised his hand and struck Jemima; but the courageous girl still grappled with him, and seeing a poniard hanging by his girdle, she, with a sudden movement, snatched it from its sheath, and held it to his heart, exclaiming—

"Advance, hired assassin, who for gold, not patriotism, would take life. Advance, I say, at your peril."

The fellow was staggered at this most unexpected resistance from such a quarter, and looked the picture of alarm. Then, with a brutal oath, he tore his sword from its sheath.

"Since you will, madam," he added, "forget that you are a woman, you cannot very well blame me for not remembering it. Your death be upon your own head."

No doubt he would have put his brutal threat into execution, but Alfred sprung forward, and arrived just in time to catch Jemima upon one arm, and cross swords with the fellow.

"Help! help! Malignants!" shouted the pursuivant. "A rescue Oh God!"

The sword of Alfred passed through his body, the hilt striking with a hollow sound against his chest ; he then fell to the ground a corpse. The cries he had uttered, though, had reached the ears of some persons, and the rapid tread of feet approaching the spot was heard. There was, in good truth, no time for deliberation. The danger was each moment becoming more imminent."

"Fly! Fly!" cried Jemima to Charles. "Fly, while we keep your enemies at bay."

"But—but Jemima," said Alfred, "I——"

"Hear me," said Charles. "One word, lady : it was I who stole into your chamber, not with a bad intent, but in seach of an asylum from similar foes to those who are now upon my track. I have longed to make this explanation, and now you can be reconciled to him who loves you. Do not follow me, Master Beaumont. I hear you have changed your name of Orme."

"Yes, my liege, but——"

"Hush, farewell.'"

Charles darted across the way, and was soon out of sight among the porches of old Westminster Hall.

CHAPTER XXII.

THE PLOT.

REDGROVE faithfully executed the extraordinary commission which he had been entrusted with by Cromwell, and when he returned he sought his master, in order to give him an account of his proceedings. Cromwell paced the room all the time that he, Redgrove, was speaking, and when he had concluded he stopped short, and casting himself into a chair, with a groan he said—"Oh, Redgrove, you have no child."

Redgrove shook his head.

"Happy, happy man! Methinks that, were I alone in the world, I could ride securely through all the storms of fate ; but, alas ! you, who know my secret cause of deep anxiety, are well aware of what I suffer. How—how—did he look in health, Redgrove ?"

"Pale and sickly. The heavy sickliness—of—of——"

"Go on."

"Dissipation."

"True, true. Most true. He will come to an early grave. Some brawl will see the end of one, who, after me might have been what I shall perchance pave the path for some other of less mark and likelihood to be."

"Brawls and their consequences, sir," added the secretary, "seem to be familiar enough to Harry Cromwell. There was a remarkable scar upon his face, which could not be forgotten by any one who had once seen it."

"Hold, hold! My boy had that scar before he became what he is. It was given him accidentally when there was some purity of purpose in his soul. No, no, Redgrove, he was not always what he is ; but yet what he is, is horrible. Let me now ask of you one favour."

"A favour, sir ? Command me, I pray you."

"No, Redgrove. I do not command one whom I have made my friend, and you are such. All I was about to say, was to beg of you never to let the name of Harry Cromwell again pass your lips to me, unless I broach the subject."

"Certainly—most certainly."

"Enough, enough. We will now talk of other matters, Redgrove. I feel certain that some formidable plot upon the part of the Royalists is in progress. Now, although your sympathies go with royalty, I feel assured that you will do your duty by me, in giving me your candid opinion. Do you not, Redgrove, think with me, from the signs of the times, that the Royalists are about to make some bold attempt to overthrow the Commonwealth ?"

" I do."

" That is honest, Redgrove. Do you know anything of a particular character ?"

" No, sir."

" Watch for me, then. When I say so to you, I know you understand me, that I do not mean you to betray anything that from your Royalist friends may come to you. That you quite understand ?"

" I do, sir, and you may depend upon such service as I can render to you. It is my duty, and—and, besides, I really begin to think that England may spare the expense, and the false glitter of royalty, and yet hold her place well among nations."

" Ah," cried Cromwell with animation, " you are a convert, and your better judgment, Redgrove, is peeping out, despite all your early predilections. You say that England may hold her place among other nations! Truly, she may. Has not the crafty and far-seeing Cardinal of France sent to me a special envoy, and rejected the overtures of the mock court of him who calls himself the second Charles. There is proof."

" Richlieu ?"

" Yes. Richlieu knows that there is a strong government in England, and there shall be, before I am a year older, yet a stronger."

With these words Cromwell left the room, and Redgrove for a time remained in deep thought. He was, from his intimate knowledge of Cromwell, quite free from the common vulgar notion, that he wished to raise himself to the kingly dignity, but that he fully intended to hold a strong and tight hand on the new parliament, he, Redgrove well knew.

" Well, well," he said, as he set about arranging his papers, " we live in troublous times, and Heaven only knows what will be the result. It's very odd, but I feel myself each day more and more of a Cromwellite. I, too, who was so staunch a cavalier."

*   *   *   *   *   *   *

It becomes necessary now, that we suffer a few days to elapse, during which no positive event of any importance took place, although all the parties squabbling in the state were sufficiently busy, in order that we should record an event that filled some persons with surprise, at the same time that it freed Cromwell from two serious evils. It will be remembered that Colonel Vernon, upon the occasion when he had encountered the mysterious grey man, immediately after the latter's last visit to Cromwell, had been not a little curious to learn when he would come again, and pendant to that information, he certainly had made up his mind to something energetic. A rather squally day was fast drawing to a close, when Vernon, in his undress uniform, was standing by the gate of St. James's, conversing with an officer who was then in command of the palace guard. This officer was the same who had received such positive orders from Cromwell to admit upon all occasions the grey man without question or comment.

" Be assured," said Colonel Vernon, " he will come to-night."

" Then you have positive information ?" said the officer, with a curious look.

" Yes, I took some pains to ascertain so much, and now you can do me the favour of giving me due notice of his approach."

" With pleasure, colonel, and I sincerely hope that you will succeed in fathoming his mystery. It don't look well at all to the troops, that the general should be visited in so odd a manner by one, concerning whom the superstitious look grave, and the rational angry."

" You take exactly my view of the transaction."

The officer bowed, as though he would imply that that was a compliment, and Colonel Vernon continued—

" You perceive yon small window with the top squares of painted glass—well, it looks to a little room opening upon the corridor, which this mysterious personage must traverse in his route to Cromwell's private cabinet. When you allow the grey man, then, to pass your post, cast up against that window, as quietly as may be, some dirt or small pebbles, or anything at hand that will strike secretly against the panes of glass."

" I can be provided."

" Certainly, I shall then know that he is coming. You will be so good, then, as to keep your attention upon the window, and if you see a pane of its glass broken, come up yourself with a couple of dragoons."

" All shall be according to your commands, colonel."

" Nay, Gresham, I talk to you now as a private friend, and not as your colonel. This is quite a confidential affair, recollect, between you and I. It is a matter of absolute necessity, that, for the safety of the state and ourselves, we should know who this visitor of the general's really is."

" And you will know to-night ?"

" Assuredly, or nothing else know in this world,"

" The thing is as good as settled, then," said the officer. " Take up your post, colonel ; you will find all your directions punctually obeyed by me in the minutest particular."

" I thank you."

Colonel Vernon then entered the palace, and making' his way up a short 'staircase, he soon reached the corridor, or gallery, as it might with equal propriety be called, from which opened the little room he had mentioned with the partially stained glass window, and which was likewise the direct route to Cromwell's private cabinet, in which he always had his interviews with the grey man. Hardly, however, had Vernon gone into the little room and closed the door, when he heard the sound of a footstep approaching, and opening the door again about the space of half an inch, he looked out. and saw that it was Redgrove.

" Hist, hist !" he cried.

The secretary looked around him in some astonishment, for he could not imagine whence the sound proceeded ; but when Vernon opened the door a little wider, and called to him, he walked up at once, saying—

" Ah, colonel, I think I know your purpose."

" No doubt of it. Will you bear me company ?"

" In intercepting the grey man ?"

" Precisely."

" I think I ought not, colonel ; I am secretary to the general only while you are an officer as well as a private friend, and may do things that would ill become me. I cannot consistently interfere in the matter, but I wish you success, and I will be close at hand to see what does happen, as you might like a witness."

" True, good Redgrove—true ; you take a correct view of this matter, my good friend, and I shall be particularly well pleased to have you within call ; for that the general has been, and is, the dupe of some clever impostor, there cannot be the shadow of a doubt."

" It must be so. You have but to raise your voice slightly, and I will come."

" Where is the general ?"

The secretary pointed down the corridor, in the direction of the private cabinet, and Vernon nodded his head, to signify that he understood that there was Cromwell ; after which, closing the door of the little room, he resolved to wait patiently until the officer should give him the signal agreed upon, of the arrival of the mysterious grey man within the precincts of the old palace of St. James's. The twilight could scarcely be said to have fairly begun, for the day was particularly dark, in consequence of the disturbed state of the elements, and General Vernon could hardly persuade himself that it was not much later than it really war. In truth he muttered—

"I shall not be a little disappointed if this fellow, with his grey face, comes not this evening." Scarcely had these words escaped his lips, when clatter came a handful of small gravel against the window panes.

" Ah! right, right," said Colonel Vernon, as he hastily left the room ; fortunate indeed, for I like not surprise, and have too much business on hand to waste my time heedlessly.   So, ho ! my grey friend, we will see what you are made of to-night."

The corridor was rather lighter than the little room, for a very large bay-window at the further end of it looked to the west, and the expiring day was concentrating its powers in that direction, and beneath the fringed edge of some murky clouds there came a broad stream of yellow light, which, penetrating the glass of the large bay-window, spread itself along the corridor.

"I shall have the advantage of him," said Colonel Vernon, "the light will be upon his face ; and, by all that's odd, here he is.   The same grey, tall, unearthly-looking figure, which we have before described to the reader, ascended, with a slow and solemn step, the stairs, and confronted Colonel Vernon within about twelve paces of the top.   The Colonel deliberately drew his sword, and giving it a graceful wave, so as to nearly command the whole width of the corridor, he said—

"Hold, sir ; you pass not here without a full and explicit declaration of your service and business."

The grey man paused, and then, in a deep hollow voice, he replied—

"Forbear, rash man ; you know not the powers you dare !"

"You may add to that—I care not," said Vernon. "It is to my interest, and to the interest of many brave men, that Cromwell should not be imposed upon by a mountebank ; and from this time henceforth the juggle is at an end."

"I have a written pass from him whom you call master."

"If you had a written pass from the devil, and another from St. Peter, they should not avail you here.   Yield yourself my prisoner, and confess your imposture, then we will see what grace can be shown to a rogue."

"Oh, fool, fool !   Know you not—guess you not—that the powers of the world that is not of earth earthly, are such, that by a breath you might be made to shrink from before me like a withered blade of last summer's grass.   To yourself be merciful, and in your silent secret thoughts, tell yourself that in an impious moment you dared, with impunity, what no man yet dared in this world of mortality and woe."

"Very good, but still you pass not."

"And if I return in obedience to your mortal mandate——"

"Why then you will be seized by my orders at the gate.   Come—come, the farce is over.   Give up this mummery, and yield yourself with the best grace you may to me.   My name is Vernon, and that ought to give you full information that you have at last met your match.   It is tolerably well known that I am no trifler."

"And must I then crush this worm ?" faintly ejaculated the grey man, as if ruminating with himself, in a tone of deep regret.

"Oh, never mind me," said Vernon, "I fully deserve it, you know.   But yet you shall not pass this corridor. The play is over, I tell you, and your occupation is gone."

A visible emotion shook the frame of the grey man, and after a moment's silence, he said—

"And yet I have in my etherial composition a spirit's pity for mortal bravery. Oh, have mercy upon yourself, proud man. Stand from before me—my touch, aye the touch even of my garments would blight the springs of life, and like some poor moth, that flitters away its little life in the sparkle of a flame that kills it, you would fall.   Oh, man, again I say have mercy upon yourself."

That may I.   But I will have none upon you. By heavens, you are a cleverer rogue than I thought to find you ; and yet I should have known that Cromwell was not to be hoodwinked by any common cheater.   At once I will test this blighting, withering quality of your garments, and if I fall like a singed moth, why then, if I can, I will own that conviction has come too late, and that I deserve my fate.

The grey man was silenced, but Colonel Vernon saw that he looked hastily to the right and to the left, as though he were seeking for some mode of escape.

His right hand, too, wandered to the hilt of a long rapier that hung by his side in a sheath covered with grey cloth. All these mundane symptoms did not escape the vigilant eye of the colonel.

"Yield!" he cried, "yield while you are in a whole skin."

The grey man now made one last effort. Drawing himself up to his full height, he said—

"Colonel Vernon, I come upon public business of importance to General Cromwell, and I command you to announce me."

' I will not."

"Then die, insolent caitiff!"

With a rapid movement, that Colonel Vernon was not at all prepared for, the mysterious stranger drew his rapier, and, springing forward like lightning, he made a full pass at Vernon's breast. Had the aim been as good as the intention, the mortal career of Colonel Vernon would then and there have come to a conclusion, but such was not the case. The rapier passed across his chest, slightly grazing his skin, and ripping up his apparel in a long slit as it flew under his arm, without doing him any further damage. With such force had this thrust been made, that the grey man was half thrown off his equilibrium for a moment, and then, before he could recover himself, the colonel's sword was sheathed in his body.

"I would have spared you," said Vernon, "but you would have it."

With a gasping sob the unhappy wretch tried to say something, but the effort was a vain one. He madly struck at Vernon with his sword, and went reeling back towards the staircase he had so recently ascended. Vernon followed, fencing with him as coolly as though nothing particular was the matter, and then, as he fully expected, when he reached the head of the stairs, the grey man paused one moment, and then falling cleanly backwards, pitched headlong down the steep descent.

"Redgrove! Redgrove!" cried Vernon.

"Here!" cried the secretary, emerging from a side room. "Have you killed him?"

"I fancy so."

"Where is he?'

"He fell down the staircase, dead, I think, before he toppled over. I never saw any one fall in such a manner in my life. Tell me truly, Redgrove, did you, or did you not, overhear the conversation that ensued between me and that foolish wretch?"

"I did!"

"By the light of day, I'm glad of that, for you know now that with singular patience I told him of his danger, and offered him mercy, but he would needs try to make me what he would fain have persuaded me he was himself."

"A ghost!"

"Precisely, Redgrove. Let us go down. Yet, stay a moment; I think we may as well have some more witnesses. I will be with you directly.

The Colonel ran into the little room again, and with the hilt of his sword smashed a window, which he knew would bring the officer on guard at the gate, with a couple of dragoons, to the foot of the stairs. He then hastily joined the secretary, and they both descended, looking carefully before them for the corpse of the man who had had the temerity to play such a part to its close so tragically. The staircase was very dark now, and they could, when they reached the foot of it, only see lying there a confused mass of something. The officer and the two soldiers arrived in a moment or two, however, and Colonel Vernon sent one of them for a light to the guard room, which in a few minutes the trooper brought.

"Now," said the colonel, "we shall, perhaps, find out who this is."

They turned the lifeless body upon its back, and then they saw that the face was covered with a closely fitting grey mask. Redgrove hastily shifted it off. The face was pallid with the hue of death, but the secretary caught the arm of Vernon, and turned pale.

" You know him ?"

" I—I—do."

" Who is it ? who is it ?"

Redgrove drew Vernon aside, and placing his mouth to his ear, he pronounced, in a voice which betrayed both emotion and alarm, the name of " Harry Cromw

---

CHAPTER XXIII.

CHARING CROSS.

" What ho ! Below there !" said a deep stern voice from the head of the stairs. " What means this confusion ? Answer me some one whom I know."

Redgrove placed his finger upon his lips for a signal to them all to be silent, and then he cried aloud—

" 'Tis I, general, I am coming—I only tarried a moment to say a word to Colonel Vernon. Trouble not yourself to descend."

" I thought," said Cromwell, for it was he, " I thought I heard the clash of swords. I am coming down, Redgrove, in a moment. Do not trouble to come up at present."

" The clash of swords, sir ?" said Redgrove ; " oh, yes, I was foolish enough to dash my own sword down the stairs. For the love of God, hide the body somewhere, Vernon."

" Yes—yes. Go up, and stop him, if it be only a moment."

Redgrove sprung up the stairs, and met Cromwell—

" Any news, sir ?" he said

" No, my good Redgrove, but my mind is much disturbed to-night. It seem as though clouds were thickening around me."

" Clouds, sir ?"

" Yes, but why do you stop my way ? Allow me to pass on, an it please you, od Redgrove."

" Oh, sir, forgive me, for quite unconsciously impeding you. I believe the colonel is below."

" Yes," said Vernon, " all's right."

The last two words were pronounced with a marked emphasis. They were intended for Redgrove, to assure him there was no longer any necessity for impeding Cromwell in descending the staircase, at the foot of which had lain the corpse of his erring but still loved son, and the secretary fully understood this. Both he and Cromwell reached the foot of the staircase together, but the latter looked, as well as he could by the dim twilight, in both their faces. The soldiers and the officer were gone.

" Humph !" said Cromwell.

It was as clear as noonday, that he was not completely hoodwinked, but that he had his suspicions something was going on which Vernon and Redgrove wished to keep from him, but, with his habitual caution and reserve, he said nothing upon the subject, so that they were not put to the disagreeable task of forging any untruths."

" All is peace !" said Cromwell.

Even as he spoke, the dull, sullen, heavy, boom of a cannon te pon thei ears—then another—then another—another still—until twenty-one had been counted by the astounded party at the foot of the little stairs.

" What is that ?" said Vernon.

" A royal salute," said Redgrove.

Cromwell started, as though cold steel had passed through his heart, and in a voice of thunder he replied—" A royal plot ! To arms ! My horse and arms,

Vernon. Sound trumpets. To horse! To horse! The clouds are breaking. Oh, Vernon, I knew that fate was big with some important secret. I felt that something was hatching, and that the dawning Commonwealth of England stood upon a mine; but, with God's help and our own strong arms, we will yet smite the malignants. To horse! To horse! I say—to horse! There will be warm work yet to-night."

*   *   *   *   *   *   *

We must now once again request the reader to stand with us upon the deck

CROMWELL AND HIS IRONSIDES CHARGE THE MOB AT CHARING CROSS.

of the Gooden Gelt, as just at sunset upon this most eventful evening, that tight built craft brought up nearer shore than would have been prudent if the tide had been flowing. About six boats were dancing in her wake, and in about a quarter of an hour they were rowed to shore, each well filled by men of most sanctimonious aspect. One of these boats landed at the nearest spot it could on the Middlesex side of the river, and its occupants, five in number, walked calmly through the city, down the Strand, and so on until they came to Charing Cross, where they all stopped at a house which stood within two doors from Spring Gardens. Some one must have been waiting in the passage of this house, for the door was opened with the most marvellous celerity, and two of the five personages went in, while the other three walked rapidly away towards what is now the Haymarket. The door was slammed to again in a moment ; but we will take the liberty of following these two persons into a comfortable apartment upon the first floor of the house, whither they at once followed the person who had let them in with such celerity the moment they had demanded admittance. The drawing-room floor of the house, to which the persons ascended, was fitted up in rather a strange fashion, for such a place. At one end of the room was a richly decorated and emblazoned arm chair, close to which was a footstool to correspond, so that there was quite a royal sort of air given to the place. The two arrivals, and the person who had opened the door, entered this room, the door of which the latter immediately locked on the inside, and then, in a subdued but clear voice, he said—

"Long live the king !"

"Long live the king !" cried one of the others. "I pray your majesty to be seated."

"Upon my faith, gentlemen," said the third person, who was no other than Charles himself, "you are perhaps a little premature, gentlemen, in this affair. I only hope that ere long there may be a king in England to cry long life to. Should there be, I can say he will endeavour to deserve the wish, my lords."

"Pardon me, your majesty," said one, "I am no lord, but plain Alfred Beaumont, and your majesty's most devoted servant. My Lord Repton here most deservedly wears and graces his title."

"Odd's-fish, man, it won't do for kings to make mistakes. You must be Lord Beaumont, and we will give our commands, if our commands are worth anything, to the proper officers, if we should chance to have any proper officers, to make out your letters and patent of nobility. By the bye—a—hem ! Have you explained yourself satisfactorily to the young lady—the draper's niece ?"

"I have, sire. But let me tell your majesty what is arranged. The Lords Wilton and Sefton, and Sir Francis Grey, with Master Wilton and the Earl of Guilford, will, at different parts of London, appear in arms with what followers they can collect, and commence each a rapid march towards Charing Cross. From a masked battery upon the banks of the river, in the gardens of Lord Repton's house, a royal salute of twenty-one guns will be suddenly fired, as a signal to commence operations, and then the movement will really begin."

"And Marston ! Where is he ?"

"Sir Philip Marston, my liege, will raise the royal standard within sight of this window, and hold his ground with two hundred followers, best he may, until the arrival of our friends, who expect to swell their ranks as they proceed."

"And when are we to appear ?"

"As soon as your majesty shall, from a knowledge of what is taking place, think proper to show your royal person, properly attired as becomes a king. Robes of state are here ready for your majesty's use, and it is hoped that your gracious approval will at once give such a tone to the affair as to decide the fortune of the fight."

"I pray that it may, my lord. But if we fail ?"

"At the worst, your majesty can hastily divest yourself of your robes, and then, by the back garden of this house, get into the park, where four of our friends wait with fleet horses, upon one of which your majesty will have no trouble in quickly reaching Chelsea, and then, at Major Hornden's house, you can take boat and get on board the Gooden Gelt, which will, upon the moment, set sail for the Scheldt."

"Well," said Charles, with a careless air, "1 will say, my lords, that this whole plan is far from being badly devised. It is, in sooth, bold and promising."

"It's boldness makes it promising," said Lord Repton ; "I must say that I am most sanguine of success. It is an excellent plot, and to-morrow's dawn will see your majesty a king in fact, as well as in right."

"Ah! what sound is that?"

Boom! came the sound of the first gun of the twenty-one—that same first gun which had startled Cromwell as he stood at the foot of the little flight of stairs, down which had fallen, headlong, the lifeless body of his erring son.

"The salute," cried Lord Repton. "Hark! Count them."

In silence the twenty-one guns were counted, and at the conclusion the new Lord Beaumont handed to Charles a royal robe of purple and carmine, which he hastily put on. They could see that his hands shook a little, but his voice was firm as he said—

"Now, my lords, I have set my life upon this cast, and I will stand the hazard of the die. Let us watch from the window the progress of events, and when the time shall come for the King of England to show himself to his people, you will not find Charles the Second backwards in doing so."

CHAPTER XXIV.

THE CONCLUSION.

As if by magic, from out of door-ways, shops, and houses, there now issued armed men, and dashing onwards from a narrow street in the immediate vicinity, there came three mounted officers in rich uniforms. One was Sir Philip Marston, another Lord Sefton, and the third Sir Charles Courtney. He, Sir Charles, carried the king's banner. After these horsemen, came two heralds in all the emblazonry of courtly state, and, blowing a rousing strain upon their trumpets, they awakened echo far and near. Then Sir Philip Marston cried in a loud clear voice—

"Long live King Charles the Second!"

A loud hurrah from the two hundred armed men, who were there to commence and form a sort of nucleus to the movement, completed its inauguration, and they formed in a dense mass around their leaders, and a snearly as possible upon the spot, where now stands the equestrian statue of Charles. The effect produced upon the surrounding locality, by this bold and most unexpected movement, was far beyond what any description can do justice to. The shops were hastily shut up. Some came with arms in their hands, hastily snatched up at the moment to join the royal cause, and then in the night air floated that standard which was thought to be for ever eclipsed in England. Confusion and cries of all kinds and descriptions began now to fill the air, and within the short space of fifteen minutes, so contagious is courage as well as fear, the royal party had around them twice their number of volunteers. It took about this fifteen minutes for Cromwell to get ready a troop of horse of about two hundred and fifty strong, and just as St. James's Palace clock struck eight, this troop galloped off in the direction of Charing Cross. Before they reached, however, the spot where the royal standard had been hoisted, Lord Wilton, with about five hundred men came down the Strand. His original force which at starting by Bridge-street, Blackfriars, had been one hundred and ten men, had thus wonderfully increased upon passing the neighbourhood of the Temple and Whitefriars. This force, looking formidable, if it were not so debauched, marched into the open space by Charing Cross at the moment that the advance guard of Cromwell's dragoons, came in sight from Pall Mall. Cromwell himself now galloped past the advance, and cast a stern scrutinizing look upon the approaching mob. Then trotting back, he pointed to them, and in a loud voice, cried—

"Halt! Front! Charge!"

Like a torrent, down came the dragoons upon Lord Wilton's party, occupying in this impetuous charge the whole of the open space. Lord Wilton rose in his stirrups, and shouted—

"Let them through your ranks! Let them through your ranks, my men! Hurrah! That will do. Long live the king! Close upon them. St. George for merry England. Hurrah!"

Not a soul, except Sir Charles Courtney, had opposed the charge of the dragoons, but every one had made what way he could for the horsemen to pass; but then the mob closed upon them, and a frightful scene of carnage ensued. Each individual soldier found himself in the midst of a little knot of foes, who were using all descriptions of offensive weapons against him. Sir Charles Courtney had alone fairly met the charge of an officer, and cut him down at once by a tremendous blow with the long straight sword he wielded. It would almost appear as if Cromwell had not seen the party in the midst of which floated the royal banner of England; but when Sir Philip Marston saw the hot work that was going on, he at once led his force to the attack, giving orders that any one who could secure a dragoon's horse had better mount at once. The melée now extended over the whole space of ground—now considered, and justly so, one of the finest spots of the metropolis—when suddenly a loud shout proclaimed the arrival by St. Giles's, of the Earl of Guilford with his force, which consisted of nearly a thousand persons; but the notes of a trumpet mingled with the shouts of the multitude, and in regular order, at a smart trot came up Cromwell's own regiment of Ironsides, consisting of eight hundred picked troopers. Gladly would they have fired at once upon the mob, but the survivors of the original two hundred and fifty troopers who had charged the people, were so mixed up with the Royalists, that they would have most probably been the greatest sufferers by the shots of their comrades. Cromwell however, who had extricated himself, by cutting down all who opposed him, from the first disastrous charge—for disastrous it was—glanced rapidly at the scene of action, and riding to the flank of the newly arrived regiment, he shouted—

"Left face. Fire!"

This had the effect of directing the fire of their carbines full upon Lord Guilford's party, which had just emerged from the mass of intricate streets about St. Giles's, and which little expected such a rattling reception. The mob paused, swayed to and fro for a moment or two, and then fled, leaving the earl with not more than twenty men around him.

"Right face!" shouted Cromwell, and again the regiment faced the original mob.

"Charge! Give no quarter to the malignants. The battle is the Lord's! Forward!"

Charles saw all that happened from the window of the new Lord Beaumont's house, and one may guess what must have been the sensations that came over him during the brief half hour which these events took to actively show themselves. Certainly, acting upon the understanding that he was, not to appear unless something sufficiently favourable took place to warrant the exhibition of his person, he could not be blamed for remaining where he was, although a more generous spirit would perhaps have not been so content to look from a window at men fighting to the death in his cause. This charge of Cromwell's regiment was decisive. Nothing could stand against it, and the mob was bodily borne down, by the weight of man and horse brought against it. "Every one for himself," was now the order of the day, and the route began. In ten minutes' time the dragoons had possession of the whole space, and the royal banner was picked up, torn into shreds by the horses' feet. Whether it was that the other leaders of the movement who were to arrive with their forces could not get them together in time, or, that hearing of what had happened at Charing Cross, they hastily disbanded them again, matters but little, for the fact that they did not make any appearance at the agreed upon scene of action was certain, and the rising from which so much was expected. Cromwell looked around him with a grim smile. "Vernon!" he said, "Vernon!"

" Here, general."

" The clouds have dispersed, and I feel myself again. Make what prisoners you can, if they seem of any note. As for the poor rabble, we are better without them. Let them go terrified to their haunts. Methinks it will be one while before the standard of revolt is raised here against the sovereign of the people."

" General, I suspect——"

" What ?"

" That Charles himself must be in London. This affair is of much too serious a character to have been undertaken without his being near at hand to profit by its success, had it turned out otherwise than what it has."

" Find him, Vernon, and sit next my heart."

Cromwell galloped off, and it was not until he nearly reached St. James's, that the officers with him saw blood dripping to the ground from a wound he had received.

" Yes, a mere scratch. 'Tis nothing," replied Cromwell hastily, to an officer who rode up to him to mention the circumstance to him. " A mere scratch—I thank you."

When, however, Cromwell dismounted from his horse, he found that, owing to copious bleeding from his wound, he was so weak that it was with difficulty he could walk ; but so much unaccustomed was he to make any complaints, that he walked on, passing the guard with a slight salute merely. The officer, however—and it was not the same one who had been mixed up in the affair of the grey man—saw that something was the matter, and after looking after the general and seeing him reel a little, he sprung forward and offered his arm, saying—

" Are you ill, sir ?"

" No—no—a slight wound. Let me rest in the nearest room, and send for the learned Doctor Turner. 1 bleed too freely, and am faint and weak. Get me a light—I—I will lean upon you, if you please. We have beaten, sir, the disturbers of the public peace. Quite beaten them."

" I'm glad of it, sir. There is a small room to the right, through this door. Guard ! guard ! a light here—a light !"

A trooper brought a light from the guard-room, and he was one of the troopers who had been engaged in the affair of the grey man, but he had not heard who the dead man was. All he was aware of was that there was some serious mystery in the matter, and that there had been a great anxiety to get the body into the little room without Cromwell being aware of what had happened. Why or wherefore this was he knew not. The officer flung the door open, and supported Cromwell towards the threshold, saying to the trooper, in a voice of authority—

" Bring in the light."

The soldier hesitated.

" Bring in the light," again cried the officer, angrily. " Do you not see that the general nearly faints ?"

The trooper no longer hesitated. Positive orders must be obeyed, and accordingly discharging from his mind all other considerations, he flung the door open and lighted Cromwell and the officer, upon whom he leant heavily, into the apartment.

" I thank you kindly," said Cromwell. " Oh ! here is a seat. I will wait the good surgeon's coming. Some rebel has had a keen blade and a strong hand to give me such a slash as this with. Well, who would have thought 'twould have bled in such a fashion ? But we have beaten them, sir—we have beaten them, sir, with the Lord's help, and England still is free from those kings who made an estate of the happy glades of this great country ! I have not, sir, the feather in my cap that appertains to royalty, but I will see right done, if the Lord will give me strength."

He sat down in the first seat he came to, and then the trooper, having placed he light upon the table, could not for the life of him forbear from casting his eyes towards the far corner of the room, where lay the stiff and blood-stained body of the grey man. The officer had gone to summon the surgeon the general had mentioned.

"Why do you fix your eyes on vacancy?" said Cromwell to the trooper.

"General—I—I——"

"Ah, knave! Dare you palter with me? Speak, I say, or, by——"

"Pardon, general, I only looked at the body."

Cromwell rose instantly, grasping the arms of the chair with both hands, as in a hoarse loud voice he said—

"What body—what body?"

"I know not, general."

"Give me the light. So—so——"

Forgetting for a moment the pain of his wound, and having a strange and new strength lent to him by the excitement of the moment, Cromwell approached the spot where the grey man lay. He held the light slightly above his head as he went, and from the first moment that his eyes fell upon the long, gaunt-looking spectacle, he did not take them off. Stooping, he went lower and lower with the light, until its full beams fell upon the dead face. For a moment he was still as a rock. Then, rising up, he threw above his head both of his hands, and uttering a cry of despair, all was intense darkness, and then the terrified soldier heard him fall to the floor like a lump of lead. The Protector now knew his secret.

* * * * * * *

This remarkable episode in the life of that most remarkable man of his age, Oliver Cromwell, is now over, and it only remains for us to state, that when Charles the Second found that really there was no hope from the rising in his favour, he divested himself of the kingly robes much more hastily than he had put them on.

"All is lost!" he cried.

"No, sir, no," said Lord Beaumont, "not all; a happier time will come."

Charles shook his head.

"The moments are precious," said Lord Repton. "Fly, Beaumont, and see that the horses for his majesty are all safe. Any failure now in that quarter would be positive and speedy destruction to us all. Fly, my lord, fly! We will follow you at once."

"My good friends," said Charles, "come with me both of you. I will go at once to the Hague, and there, collecting around me such of my own and my father's old friends as I know to be staunch and true, I will wait until some more favourable train of circumstances shall call me to fill that throne, the struggle for the possession of which shall cease only with my life. I have but one deep-seated sadness now at my heart, and that is, for the unavailing blood that has been shed to-night. Come, my lords, come!"

In one hour after, the Gooden Gelt was under weigh; and while Charles sat in the cabin in a moody silence, Sir Charles Courtney and Lord Beaumont were conversing together upon the deck, while their respective ladies—Mary, the Puritan's daughter, and Jemima, the niece of Dashall—were taking what they thought might be a last look at England from the vessel's deck.

FINIS.